THE THREE MUSKETEERS

CHILDREN'S
CLASSICS

THE THREE MUSKETEERS

Alexander Dumas

Bloomsbury Books
London

This edition published 1994 by Bloomsbury Books, an imprint of The Godfrey Cave Group, 42 Bloomsbury Street, London, WC1B 3QJ.

ISBN 1 85471 245 4

Printed and bound by Imprimerie Hérissey, France.

No d'impression : 25065

Contents

1

A Troubled Start

On the first Monday of the month of April, 1625, the small town of Meung appeared to be in a state of revolution. Many of the townsmen were proceeding towards the inn of the Jolly Miller, to which a vast and increasing mob was hastening with intense curiosity.

At that period in France alarms were frequent. The nobles made war on each other; there was the king, who made war on the cardinal; there was the Spaniard who made war on the king.

Having reached the inn everyone could see and understand the cause of this alarm—a young man clothed in a woollen doublet, whose blue colour was faded to an indistinguishable shade between the lees of wine and a cerulean blue; the face long and brown; the cheekbones high, denoting acuteness; the muscles of the jaw enormously developed—an infallible mark by which a Gascon may be recognized, even without the cap, and our youth wore a cap, adorned with a sort of feather; the eye full and intelligent; the nose hooked but finely formed; the whole figure too large for a youth, yet too small for an adult.

Our youth had a steed, and this steed was at the same time so remarkable as to attract observation. It was a Béarnese sheltie, of about twelve or fourteen years of age, yellow as an orange, without any hair on its tail, but abundance of galls on its legs.

The young man's name was d'Artagnan. His father had given him the horse when he had set out for Paris from his home at Tarbes in Gascony and had also handed him a letter of introduction to M. de Tréville, an old friend, now captain of the king's musketeers. His mother had given him a recipe for a certain balm which had miraculous healing powers for wounds that did not touch the heart.

Furnished with these paternal gifts, the young d'Artagnan set out for Paris and, with sword of respectable length and sternly glistening eye, made dignified progress as far as the fatal town of Meung. There for the first time, he overheard a gentleman with a distinguished air making fun of his horse from the Jolly Miller inn.

Now, since even the slightest smile was sufficient to rouse the anger of our youth, we may well imagine what effect such unbounded mirth was likely to produce upon him. Nevertheless, d'Artagnan wished first to examine the countenance of the impertinent fellow who thus laughed at him, and saw a man from forty to forty-five years of age, with eyes black and piercing, complexion pale, nose strongly marked and moustache black and carefully trimmed. He was attired in a violet-coloured doublet and breeches, with points of the same colour, with no other ornament than the slashes through which the shirt appeared. An instinct told d'Artagnan that this unknown was to have a vast influence on his future life.

At the very moment that d'Artagnan fixed his eyes upon the man in the violet doublet, that individual made one of his wisest and most profound remarks upon the Béarnese horse.

"I say, sir!" d'Artagnan cried; "you, sir, who hide yourself behind the shutter—yes, you, sir, tell me what you are laughing at and we will laugh together!"

The gentleman slowly turned his eyes from the steed to its rider and made some sarcastic remarks about the horse's master.

He had scarcely finished when d'Artagnan made such a furious thrust at him, that, had he not jumped back briskly, it is probable the jest would have been his last. Perceiving now, however, that the affair was beyond a joke, the unknown drew his sword, saluted his adversary, and gravely put himself on guard; but at the same moment his two companions, accompanied by the host, fell pell-mell upon d'Artagnan with sticks, shovels and tongs. D'Artagnan was not a man ever to cry for quarter; the fight was therefore prolonged, until at last, completely worn out, he dropped his sword, which was broken in two by a blow from a stick, while at the same instant another blow, which cut open his forehead, stretched him on the ground almost senseless.

It was now that all the burghers hastened to the scene of the action. Fearing a disturbance, the landlord, assisted by his servants, carried the wounded man into the kitchen, where some care was given him. As for the stranger in the violet doublet, he returned to the window and viewed the crowd with evident marks of impatience, seeming rather annoyed at their refusal to go away.

"Well, how is the madman now?" said he, turning, and addressing the host, who came to inquire in what state his guest was.

"Is your Excellency safe and well?" demanded the host.

"Yes, perfectly so, mine host; but a wish to know what is become of this youth."

"He is better," replied the host, "but he is quite senseless."

"Indeed!" said the gentleman.

"But before he quite lost his senses, he rallied all his strength to challenge and defy you," added the landlord.

"Well, this young fellow is the very devil himself," said the gentleman.

"Oh, no, your Excellency," replied the host with a contemptuous grin, "he is not the devil, for while he was senseless we rummaged his outfit, and in his bundle we found but one shirt, and in his pocket only twelve crowns and a letter, addressed to M. de Tréville, captain of the musketeers."

"The devil!" muttered the gentleman between his teeth. "Could de Tréville have set this Gascon upon me? He is very young; but a thrust of a sword is a thrust of a sword, whatever may be the age of him who gives it, and one distrusts a boy less than an oldster; a slight obstacle is sufficient to thwart a project."

And the stranger fell into a reverie that lasted some minutes. After that he called out:

"Host, go, make out my bill and call my servants."

"What, sir, must you be off?"

"Yes, I ordered you to saddle my horse; have I not been obeyed?"

"Yes; your Excellency may see your horse standing under the great gateway, quite ready for the road."

"Very well; then do as I have ordered."

"Heyday!" said the host to himself. "Can he be afraid of this young boy?"

"My lady must not see this strange fellow," said the stranger. "As she is already late, she must soon pass by. I had better mount my horse and go to meet her. If I could only just learn the contents of that letter addressed to Tréville." And he descended to the kitchen.

In the meantime, the landlord found that d'Artagnan had regained consciousness and persuaded him, in spite of his weakness, to resume his journey.

D'Artagnan, half stunned, without doublet, his head completely bandaged, arose, but on reaching the kitchen the first thing he saw was his opponent, who was quietly talking at the step of a heavy carriage to a woman of from twenty to twenty-two years of age, whose head appeared, through the window of the carriage, like a picture in a frame. D'Artagnan saw that the lady was young and attractive. Now, this beauty was the more striking to him as it was completely different from that of his own southern country. She was pale, and fair, with long curls falling on her shoulders, large blue languishing eyes, rosy lips and alabaster hands. She conversed with the unknown with great vivacity.

"So, his eminence commands me—" said she.

"To return immediately to England, and inform him, with all speed, if the duke leaves London."

"And as to my other instructions?" demanded the fair traveller.

"They are enclosed in this box, which you will not open until you are on the other side of the Channel."

"Good; and you? What are you going to do?"

"I return to Paris."

"Without chastising this insolent boy?" demanded the lady.

The unknown was about to reply, but at that very moment d'Artagnan, who had heard every word, rushed through the open door. "This insolent boy," he cried, "chastises others, and I hope that this time he who deserves chastisement will not escape him."

"Will not escape him?" echoed the unknown, knitting his brows.

"No, in the presence of a woman you would hesitate to fly, a presume.

"Remember," said the lady, seeing the gentleman place his hand on his sword, "that the slightest delay may ruin us all."

"You are right," said the gentleman; "you go your way, and I will go mine;' and saluting the lady with a bow, he got into the saddle, whilst the coachman whipped up his horses. The lady and gentleman therefore went off at a gallop in opposite directions.

Thanks, no doubt, to his mother's salve, and perhaps also the absence of any doctor, d'Artagnan found himself almost cured by the next day. But at the moment he was paying for wine, oil and rosemary, the ingredients of the balm, he found nothing in his pocket but his little purse. The letter to M. de Tréville was gone. The young man began by looking very patiently for this letter, turning out and rummaging in his pockets and fobs twenty times, rummaging in his valise again and again, and opening and shutting his purse; but when he was quite convinced that the letter was not to be found, he gave full vent to another fit of rage in a manner which was like to make necessary a second decoction of wine and spiced oil. A sudden flash of light illumined the mind of the host.

"That letter is not lost!" he cried. "It has been stolen from you."

"Stolen! And by whom?"

"By the stranger, yesterday; he went into the kitchen where your doublet was lying; he was there for a time entirely alone; and I will lay a wager it was he who stole it from you."

"You really think so?" said d'Artagnan, and majestically he drew from his pocket two crowns which he handed to the host, who followed him cap in hand, to the gateway. There he remounted his yellow horse, which carried him without further accident to the gate of St. Antoine at Paris, where its owner sold the animal for three crowns; which was a good price, considering that d'Artagnan had ridden him hard on the last part of the journey.

D'Artagnan therefore entered Paris on foot, carrying his small valise under his arm, and walked around until he found a lodging suitable to his slender resources. It was a sort of garret, situated in the Rue des Fossoyeurs, near the Luxembourg. He learned from the first musketeer he met where M. de Tréville's house was situated, which proved to be in the very neighbourhood where he had himself taken up his abode.

Next morning he repaired to the residence of the famous man.

M. de Troisville, as his family was yet called in Gascony, or M. de Tréville, as he called himself in Paris, had actually begun life like d'Artagnan; that is to say, without being worth a sou, but with a Gascon fund of audacity, shrewdness and resolution. He was admitted to the household of Louis XIII before he became king, and on his protégé ascending the throne, was appointed captain of the musketeers, whose devotion to Louis XIII was fanatical. There were always many of these musketeers at M. de Tréville's and, on the day when d'Artagnan presented himself, they made a great impression on him. Quite overawed, he gave his name modestly and was told his request for an audience of M. de Tréville would be granted in due time.

D'Artagnan, who had of course, not missed the gossip, scandal, and political discussions going on around him, now had time to study the dresses and countenances of those about him. In the midst of the most animated group was a musketeer of great height, of a haughty countenance and so fantastical a costume as to attract general attention. He did not wear his uniform cloak, which was not absolutely indispensable at that period of less liberty, yet greater independence, but a close doublet of celestial blue, slightly faded and worn, and on this coat a magnificent border of gold embroidery which glittered like scales upon a sunlit stream; a long mantle or cloak of crimson velvet hung gracefully from his shoulders, disclosing the front alone of his splendid belt, from which depended his enormous rapier. This musketeer, who had just come off guard, complained of having caught cold, and coughed occasionally with great affectation. Everyone much admired the embroidered belt, and d'Artagnan more than anyone else.

"What do you expect?" said the musketeer. "It is the fashion; I know that it is foolish, but it is the fashion; besides, one must spend one's inheritance on something or other."

"Ah, Porthos," cried one of the bystanders, "don't try to make us believe that this belt comes from paternal generosity! It was given to you by the veiled lady with whom a met you the other Sunday, near the gate of St. Honoré."

"No, upon my honour, and by the faith of a gentleman, I bought it with my own money," said he whom they called Porthos.

"Yes, as I bought this new purse with what my mistress put in the old," cried another musketeer.

"But it is true", said Porthos, "and the proof is that I paid twelve pistoles for it."

The wonder and admiration were redoubled, though the doubt still registered.

"Is it not so, Aramis?" inquired Porthos, turning to another musketeer.

The person thus appealed to formed a perfect contrast to the one who thus questioned him. He was a young man, not more than twenty-two or twenty-three years of age, with a soft and ingenuous countenance, a black mild eye, and cheeks rosy and damask as autumn peach; his slender moustache marked a perfect straight line along his upper lip; he seemed to dread to lower his hands for fear of making their veins swell; and he was continually pinching the tips of his ears, to make them preserve a delicate and transparent carnation hue. Habitually he talked little and slowly, often bowed, laughed quietly, merely showing his teeth, which were good, and of which, as of the rest of his person, he appeared to take the greatest care. He replied to his friend's question by an affirmative inclination of the head which settled all doubt.

They were interrupted by the cry of the lackey.

"M. de Tréville awaits M. d'Artagnan."

At this declaration, during which the door remained open, everyone was silent; and in the midst of this general silence the young Gascon, passing through part of the antechamber, entered the apartment of the captain of the musketeers.

M. de Tréville was at this moment in a very bad humour. He went towards the antechamber, and making a sign with his hand to d'Artagnan, as if requesting permission to finish with the others before he began with him, he called three times, raising his voice each time so as to run through the immediate scale between the tone of command and that of anger. "Athos! Porthos! Aramis!" The two musketeers, whose acquaintance we have already made, and who answered to the two last of these names, immediately quitted the group of which they formed a part.

When the two musketeers had entered, and the door was closed behind them, M. de Tréville furiously upbraided them for allowing themselves to be arrested by some of Cardinal Richelieu's guards after a brawl in the nearby Rue Ferou. But when they told him they had killed one of

their opponents his anger lessened, especially when he learned that Athos had been wounded.

At this moment the door opened, and a noble and beautiful face, but frightfully pale, appeared.

"Athos!" exclaimed the two musketeers.

"Athos!" repeated M. de Tréville.

"You sent for me, sir," said Athos, to M. de Tréville, in a perfectly calm but feeble voice. "My comrades informed me that you commanded my presence, and I hastened to obey you; here I am, sir; what do you want me for?" And with these words the musketeer, perfectly arrayed, and belted as usual, entered the room with a firm step.

M. de Tréville, touched to the heart by this proof of endurance, sprang towards him. "I was just going to tell these gentlemen," added he, "that I forbid my musketeers to expose their lives unnecessarily; for brave men are dear to the king, and he knows that his musketeers are the bravest on the earth. Your hand, Athos!" And without waiting till he responded to this proof of affection, M. de Tréville seized his hand, and pressed it with much warmth, without observing that Athos, notwithstanding his command over himself, uttered a cry of pain, and became paler than before, if that were possible. He had rallied all his powers to struggle against his pain during the interview; but he could now no longer sustain it, and fell senseless upon the carpet.

"A surgeon!" cried M. de Tréville; "mine—or rather the king's—a surgeon, the best that can be found!—or my brave Athos will die!"

At these exclamations of M. de Tréville, everyone rushed into the room, and before he could stop them, pressed round the wounded man. Forcing his way through the spectators the surgeon, who had chanced to be in the building, approached Athos, who was still insensible; and directed that the musketeer should be instantly conveyed into an adjoining apartment. M. de Tréville immediately opened a door, and pointed out the way to Porthos and Aramis, who bore off their comrade in their arms.

Upon a signal from M. de Tréville, everyone who had entered the room with the surgeon now retired except d'Artagnan, who did not abandon his audience, but with true Gascon tenacity held his ground.

"Pardon," said M. de Tréville, smiling, "pardon, my dear countryman, but I had entirely forgotten you. A captain is merely the father of a family, but burdened with a heavier responsibility than an ordinary parent: for soldiers are great children; but as I maintain that it is my duty to see that the orders of the king, and more especially those of the cardinal, are carefully executed—"

D'Artagnan could not repress a smile; and this smile satisfied M. de Tréville that he was not dealing with a fool. Therefore, he came at once to the point, and, at the same time, changed the subject.

"I loved your father," said he. "What can I do for his son? Tell me quickly, for my time is not my own."

"Sir," said d'Artagnan, "in quitting Tarbes, and coming here, a wished to ask from you, as a memorial of the friendship which you have not forgotten, the uniform of a musketeer; but from what I have seen during these last two hours, I more fully comprehend the extreme value of the favour, and tremble lest I may not be deemed a fit recipient."

"It is in fact a great favour, young man," said M. de Tréville; "but it may not be so far above you as you believe. However, his Majesty has provided a decision for this case; and I regret to inform you that no one is received among the musketeers who has not passed the ordeal of some campaigns, performed certain brilliant actions, or served for two years in some less favoured regiment than our own. I will this day write a letter to the Director of the Royal Academy, who will admit you tomorrow without any fee. Do not refuse this trifling favour. Gentlemen of the highest rank and wealth often solicit it without being able to obtain at. You will there learn to ride, to fence, and to dance; you will make some good acquaintances; and from time to time you must personally apprise me of your progress, and let me know if I can do anything for you."

D'Artagnan, ignorant as he was of the manners of high society, felt the coldness of this reception. "Alas, sir," said he, "I now feel deeply the want of the letter of introduction which my father gave me for you."

"I am, in truth, somewhat surprised," replied M. de Tréville, "that you should have undertaken so long a journey without that viaticum, so essential to every Béarnese."

"I had one, sir, and a good one—thank God!" cried d'Artagnan, "but was perfidiously robbed of it;' and with a warmth and truthfulness which charmed M. de Tréville, he recounted his adventure at Meung, accurately describing his unknown adversary.

"Tell me, had not this gentleman a slight scar on the cheek?"

"Yes, as if left by a pistol-ball."

"Was he not a man of commanding air?"

"Yes."

"Tall?"

"Yes."

"With an olivine complexion?"

"Yes, yes, that is he; but do you know this man, sir?Ah, if I ever meet him, and I will find him, I swear to you, even were he in hell—"

"He was waiting for a woman, was he not?" continued M. de Tréville.

"At least he departed after he had conversed a moment with the one he was waiting for."

"Do you know the subject of their conversation?"

"He gave her a box which he said contained her instructions, and desired her not to open it until she arrived in London."

"Was this woman an Englishwoman?"

"He called her 'my lady'."

"It is he," murmured M. de Tréville: "it must be; I thought he was at Brussels."

"Oh, sir," exclaimed d'Artagnan, "if you know this man, tell me who and whence he is, and I will hold you absolved even of your promise to admit me amongst the musketeers; for above everything else I long to avenge myself."

"Beware, young man," said M. de Tréville. "Should you perceive this man walking on the one side of the street, instead of seeking your revenge, proceed yourself on the opposite side; do not cast yourself against such a rock, upon which assuredly you will be shattered like glass."

"That fear will not deter me, should I ever meet him," said d'Artagnan.

"In the meantime, do not seek him," replied M. de Tréville. "If you take my advice—;' He broke off—he had a sudden suspicion of this young man. Was he an agent of the cardinal?

But d'Artagnan's answers to further questions allayed all further doubts on his part. M. de Tréville grasped d'Artagnan's hand and said to him: "You are an honest fellow; but at present I can only do for you what I have promised. In the meantime, my house shall always be open to you; so that having access to me at all times, and being ready to take advantage of every opportunity, you will probably hereafter obtain what you desire."

"That is to say," replied d'Artagnan, "that you will wait until I have become worthy of it. Very well," he added with Gascon familiarity, "rest assured that you will not have to wait long." And he bowed to retire, as if the future lay with himself.

"But wait a moment," said M. de Tréville, stopping him. "I promised you a letter to the Director of the Academy. Are you too proud to accept it, young gentleman?"

"No, sir," replied d'Artagnan, "and I will answer for it that the same fate that overtook my father's letter shall not occur to this. I shall take good care that it shall reach its destination; and woe be to him who should attempt to deprive me of it."

M. de Tréville smiled at this gasconade, and leaving his young countryman in the embrasure of the window where they had been talking, he sat down to write the promised letter of introduction.

M. de Tréville, having written the letter and sealed it, approached the young man to give it to him; but at the very moment when d'Artagnan held out his hand to receive it, M. de Tréville was astonished to see his protégé spring up, redden with anger, and rush out of the room, exclaiming:

" 'Od's blood! He shall not escape me this time!"

"And who is he?" demanded M. de Tréville.

"It is *he*—the thief!" replied d'Artagnan. "Oh, what a traitor!" and he vanished.

"Deuce take the madman!" murmured M. de Tréville. "Unless it is, after all, a clever mode of giving me the slip; seeing that he has failed in his purpose."

Rushing through the antechamber d'Artagnan ran full tilt against Athos, hitting his shoulder violently, and made him utter a cry, or rather a howl of pain. After some sharp hurried words they agreed to fight a duel at twelve o'clock, near the Carmes-Deschaux; then d'Artagnan rushed outside. In the street as he ran on, still hoping to catch the unknown, he had the misfortune to become enveloped in the cloak of a huge musketeer whom he discovered was Porthos.

Instead of letting the flaps go, Porthos pulled it towards him so that d'Artagnan rolled himself up in the folds and dragged the cloak away from Porthos' body. Thus it was revealed that Porthos's belt glittered with gold at the front but was only plain at the back. Even in his haste d'Artagnan could not resist making a joke about it, at which Porthos foamed with rage, and within moments they had agreed to fight a duel behind the Luxembourg at one o'clock. Still intent on his search, d'Artagnan came upon Aramis, talking with some friends. He had no desire to alienate him as well, but noticing that Aramis had his foot on a handkerchief, he drew it out and handed it to him. It happened, however, to be decorated with a coronet and coat of arms, and the others chaffed Aramis, knowing that they were the arms of Madame de Bois-Tracy. Aramis hastily denied all knowledge of the handkerchief, but when he was alone with d'Artagnan he upbraided him for being a fool and dishonouring a lady's name, explaining that he had purposely had his foot on the handkerchief. After some quarrelsome words they arranged to meet at two o'clock, at the house of M. de Tréville for a duel. Thus d'Artagnan had three duels to fight within two hours—meanwhile, his enemy had eluded him.

2

D'Artagnan Meets the King

D'Artagnan was friendless in Paris. He therefore went to meet Athos without a second, having made up his mind to be satisfied with those chosen by his adversary. Besides, he fully intended to offer the brave musketeer all suitable apologies, but, at the same time, to betray no appearance of timidity or weakness.

Full of these ideas, he sped as if on wings towards the monastery of the Carmes Deschaux—a building without windows adjoining a chapel surrounded by barren meadows, which generally served as a rendezvous for those combatants who had no time to lose. As d'Artagnan came in sight of the small open space in front of the monastery, twelve o'clock was striking and Athos had already been about five minutes on the ground.

Athos, who still suffered severely from his wound, although it had again been dressed by M. de Tréville's surgeon, had seated himself on a large stone, where he awaited his adversary with that air of calmness and dignity which never forsook him. As d'Artagnan approached, he arose and politely advanced some steps to meet him; whilst d'Artagnan, on his part, went towards his antagonist with his hat in his hand, bowing until his plume touched the ground.

Athos explained that his seconds were late, while d'Artagnan admitted that, having reached Paris only the day before, he knew no one to act as his seconds. Athos told d'Artagnan that his shoulder still hurt him abominably, at which the young Gascon offered to lend him some of his mother's balsam and suggested they fight in three days' time when his wound would be healed. This speech pleased Athos but he replied that they had to fight at once in case the news got to the cardinal's ears.

And as he spoke the gigantic form of Porthos was seen at the end of the Rue de Vaugirard.

"What!" exclaimed d'Artagnan; "is M. Porthos one of your seconds?"

"Yes. Have you any objection to him?"

"Oh, certainly not!"

"And here is the other."

D'Artagnan looked in the direction indicated by Athos and beheld Aramis.

"What!" cried he, in a tone of yet greater astonishment; "is M. Aramis your other second?"

"Certainly; are you not aware that one of us is rarely seen without the others, and that amongst the musketeers and guards at court and in the town, we are known as Athos, Porthos and Aramis, or the Three Inseparables? But as you come from Dax or Pau—"

"From Tarbes," said d'Artagnan.

"—you may very naturally be ignorant of all this."

"Really, gentlemen," said d'Artagnan, "you are well named; and should my adventure become known, it will at least prove that like draws to like."

In the meantime Porthos approached, shook hands with Athos, and turning towards d'Artagnan, stopped in astonishment.

We may mention in passing that he had changed his belt and laid aside his cloak.

"It is with this gentleman that I am about to fight," said Athos, pointing towards d'Artagnan, and at the same time saluting him.

"I too am going to fight him," replied Porthos.

"But not till one o'clock," interrupted d'Artagnan.

"And I—I am going to fight him," said Aramis, who had come up just after Porthos.

"Our appointment, however, is for two o'clock," replied d'Artagnan, with the same coolness.

"And what are you going to fight about, Athos?" demanded Aramis.

"Upon my word, I don't really know, except that he hurt my shoulder. And you, Porthos?"

"I fight because I fight," replied Porthos, colouring.

Athos, whom nothing escaped, perceived a sly smile curling the lips of the Gascon.

"We had a dispute about dress," said d'Artagnan.

"And you, Aramis?" demanded Athos.

"Me? I fight on account of a theological dispute," answered Aramis, making a sign to d'Artagnan that he wished him to conceal the true cause of their duel.

"Really!" said Athos, who observed d'Artagnan smile again.

"Yes, a passage of St. Augustine on which we could not agree," said the Gascon.

"Decidedly he is a man of spirit," murmured Athos.

"And now that you are all arrived, gentlemen, permit me to offer my apologies," said d'Artagnan.

A frown passed over the brow of Athos, a haughty smile glided over the lips of Porthos, and a negative sign was the reply of Aramis.

"You do not understand me, gentlemen," said d'Artagnan, elevating his head, on which a sunbeam played, gilding its fine and manly lines. "I wish to apologise because it is improbable that I shall be able to pay my debt to all three; for M. Athos has the right to kill me first, which greatly decreases the value of your bill, M. Porthos, whilst it renders yours, M. Aramis, almost worthless. Therefore, gentlemen, on that account alone, I again repeat my offer of apology. And now upon your guard!"

And with the most gallant and fearless mien he drew his sword.

But the two rapiers had scarcely met, when a party of the cardinal's guards, commanded by M. de Jussac, appeared at the corner of the monastery.

"The cardinal's guards!" exclaimed Porthos and Aramis at the same moment. "Sheathe swords, gentlemen—sheathe swords!"

But it was too late; the combatants had been seen in a position which left no doubt of their intentions.

"Hollo!" cried Jussac, advancing towards them and giving a signal to his men to do the same. "Hollo, musketeers! What, fighting here? And the edicts—are they forgotten, eh?"

"You are very generous, gentlemen of the guards," said Athos in a tone of the most bitter animosity, for Jussac had been one of the aggressors on the night before last. "If we saw you fighting, I promise you that we should not prevent you; therefore, let us alone, and you will enjoy the spectacle without any of the pain."

"Gentlemen," answered Jussac, "it is with regret I declare that what you request is impossible. Duty must take precedence of everything else. Sheathe, therefore, if you please, and follow us.

"Sir," said Aramis, parodying Jussac's manner, "if it depended upon ourselves we should accept your polite invitation with the utmost pleasure; but unfortunately the thing is impossible. M. de Tréville has forbidden it. Move on, therefore; it is the best thing you can do."

This mockery exasperated Jussac. "We will charge you," he said "if you disobey."

"They are five," said Athos in a low voice, "and we are only three; we shall be beaten again, and we must die here; for I positively swear that I will not again appear before the captain a vanquished man."

Athos, Porthos and Aramis closed up to each other, whilst Jussac drew up his men. This moment of delay sufficed for d'Artagnan to form his resolution. It was a choice, once made, which must be adhered to. To fight was to disobey the law, to risk his head, and by one blow to make an enemy of a minister more powerful than the king himself. All this the young man plainly perceived, and we must do him the justice to declare that he did not hesitate a single instant.

"Gentlemen," said he, "you must allow me to correct one thing which you have said. You affirmed that you were but three; but it appears to me that there are four of us."

"But you are not one of us," said Porthos.

"Gentlemen," said d'Artagnan, "only try me and I pledge you my honour that I will not leave this spot except as a conqueror."

"What is your name, my fine fellow?" said Athos.

"D'Artagnan, sir."

"Well then, Athos, Porthos, Aramis, and d'Artagnan, forward!" exclaimed Athos.

And the nine combatants rushed upon each other with a fury which did not, however, exclude a kind of method. Athos took Cahusac, one of the cardinal's favourites; Porthos selected Biscarat; and Aramis found himself opposed to two adversaries. As for d'Artagnan, he sprang towards Jussac himself.

D'Artagnan fought like a mad tiger; Jussac had had much practice, yet it took all his skill to defend himself against an adversary who departed every instant from received rules. Losing patience, he began to make mistakes. After a fierce struggle, d'Artagnan ran Jussac through and he fell wounded. The guards were forced to surrender after a savage combat, only Biscarat remaining on his feet. One of the cardinal's men was dead, the three wounded were carried to the monastery. The musketeers then rang the bell, and confiscating four out of the five swords, they set off, intoxicated with joy, towards M. de Tréville's. They walked arm in arm, occupying the whole breadth of the street; and as they accosted every musketeer they met, the march soon became a triumphal procession. D'Artagnan's heart was in a delirium of exultation, as he marched between Athos and Porthos.

"If I am not yet a musketeer," said he to his new friends, as they passed through M. de Tréville's gateway, "I am at least next door to one. Is it not so?"

The affair made a great noise. M. de Tréville strongly censured his musketeers in public; but privately, they heard only his congratulations. As, however, it was essential no time should be lost in gaining the king, M. de Tréville hastened to the Louvre. But he was too late; the king was closeted with the cardinal. However, in the evening he saw the king who was quite openly delighted with the news, although he dared not make this public. He ordered that the three friends and d'Artagnan should appear before him at noon the next day, and enter the Louvre by the private staircase. M. de Tréville smiled at the mention of the private staircase, but conceiving that he had already secured an important advantage, by thus inducing the pupil to rebel against his master, he respectfully saluted the king, and, with his permission, withdrew.

As they were not to see the king until twelve o'clock, and Athos had engaged to meet Porthos and Aramis at a tennis court, near the Luxembourg stables, to have a game of tennis, he invited d'Artagnan to join them. Although ignorant of the game, which he had never played, d'Artagnan accepted the invitation, not knowing what otherwise to do with his time in the interval. Porthos and Aramis were already there, knocking the balls about. Athos, who was very skilful in all athletic games, went to one side with d'Artagnan, and challenged them. But at the first movement which he made, although he played with his left hand he found that his wound was too recent to permit such an exertion. D'Artagnan, therefore, remained alone; and as he declared he was too unskilful to play a regular game, they only sent the balls about, without counting the points. D'Artagnan politely saluted Porthos and Aramis, declaring that he would not renew the game until he was up to their standard, and then took his station near the ropes and in the gallery.

Unfortunately for d'Artagnan, amongst the spectators there was one of the cardinal's guards who was irritated by the previous night's defeat of his companions, and had resolved to take the first opportunity of avenging it. He now believed this opportunity had arrived and made disparaging remarks about d'Artagnan. The man was Bernajoux, a notoriously quarrelsome man, and the two soon withdrew to fight a duel, unnoticed by the others.

Eventually, Bernajoux, rushing blindly upon him, spitted himself on d'Artagnan's sword. The noise attracted supporters from both sides, but soon the musketeers drove off their enemies, and hurried towards M. de Tréville's. He, already aware of this fresh disturbance, awaited their arrival.

"Quick," said he, "to the Louvre, without losing one moment! Let us endeavour to see the king before the cardinal prejudices him. We will narrate the affair as a consequence of the affair of yesterday, and the two will be disposed of together."

M. de Tréville, accompanied by the four young men, hastened towards the Louvre; but to the great surprise of the captain of the musketeers, he was informed that the king had gone stag hunting in the forest of St. Germain. M. de Tréville required this intelligence to be twice repeated, and each time his companions observed his brow become darker.

"Had his Majesty formed the intention of hunting yesterday?" he demanded.

"No, your Excellency," replied the valet. "The master of the hounds came this morning to announce that he had roused a stag; at first the king said he would not go, but subsequently he could not resist the pleasure which the chase promised him, and he set out after dinner."

"And has the king seen the cardinal?" demanded M. de Tréville.

"In all probability," replied the valet, "for this morning a saw the horses harnessed to the cardinal's carriage; I inquired where it was going, and was told to St. Germain."

"We are anticipated," said M. de Tréville. "I shall see the king this evening; but as for you, I would counsel you at present not to attempt it."

Meanwhile, M. de Tréville paid a call on the wounded Bernajoux, who was lying between life and death at his home and had no idea for the moment of concealing the the truth; and from him he heard the truth.

At about six o'clock, M. de Tréville announced his intention of proceeding to the Louvre; but as the original hour of audience was past, instead of obtaining admission by the private staircase, he placed himself in the antechamber, with the four young men. The king was not yet returned from hunting; but our friends had scarcely waited half an hour amongst the crowd of courtiers, before the doors were opened and his Majesty was announced.

Louis XIII appeared followed by his attendants. He was attired in his hunting dress, still covered with dust; he was heavily booted, and in his hand he held his riding-whip. At the first glance, d'Artagnan perceived that the king was in a violent rage.

"The aspects are unfavourable," said Athos, smiling; "we shall not be knighted this time."

"Wait here ten minutes," said M. de Tréville, "and if I do not return to you in that time, proceed to my house as it will be useless for you to wait longer for me."

The young men waited ten minutes, a quarter of an hour, even twenty minutes; and then, finding that M. de Tréville did not return, they departed, very uneasy with the turn things were taking.

M. de Tréville, who had boldly entered the royal presence, found his Majesty in a very bad humour; he was seated in an armchair, venting his irritation by striking his boots with the handle of his whip. This, however, M. de Tréville did not appear to notice, but with the utmost composure he inquired after his Majesty's health. The king, after complaining about misfortune on the hunting field, accused M. de Tréville's men of riotous behaviour. M. de Tréville tactfully reminded him of his pride in being called Louis the Just and declared this version of the tale was not true. The king admitted he was giving the cardinal's version of the story. M. de Tréville declared that the cardinal had been misinformed and the truth was very different.

He promised to return with the musketeers at seven o'clock next day. Early the next morning therefore M. de Tréville returned to the Louvre and was admitted into the king's presence. The moment that he opened the door the three musketeers and d'Artagnan, conducted by La Chesnaye, the king's confidential valet, appeared at the top of the stairs.

"Come, my brave fellows!" said the king. "I must scold you!"

The musketeers approached, bowing, d'Artagnan following behind.

"How the devil!" continued the king. "Seven of his Eminence's guards disabled by you in two days! It is too many, gentlemen; it is too many; at this rate, his Eminence will have to renew his regiment in three weeks, and I shall have to enforce the edicts in their full rigour. I say nothing of one by chance; but seven in two days, I repeat, are too many, a great deal too many!"

"But your Majesty perceives that they have come in sorrow and repentance to excuse themselves."

"In sorrow and repentance! Hum!" said the king. "I do not put much trust in their hypocritical faces. There is, in particular, a Gascon face in the background there! Come here, you, sir!"

D'Artagnan, who perceived that the compliment was addressed to him, approached his Majesty with a desperately desponding look.

"What! You told me it was a young man! But this is a mere boy, Tréville, quite a boy. Did he give that terrible wound to Jussac?"

"Yes, and those two beautiful sword thrusts to Bernajoux," said M. de Tréville.

D'Artagnan, bidden by the king, told all the circumstances of the adventure.

"You have taken your revenge for the Rue Férou," declared the king, "and more than enough. You ought to be satisfied."

"So we are, if your Majesty is," said M. de Tréville.

"Yes, I am!" replied the king, and taking a handful of gold from La Chesnaye, and giving it to d'Artagnan he added, "There is proof of my satisfaction."

At this period, the independent notions which are now current were not yet in fashion. a gentleman received money from the king's hand without being humiliated. D'Artagnan, therefore, put the forty pistoles into his pocket, without any other ceremony than that of warmly thanking his Majesty for the gift.

"Tréville," added the king in a low voice, as the others retired, "as you have no commission vacant in the musketeers, place this young man in the company of guards commanded by your brother-in-law, M. des Essarts. Ah! I quite enjoy the thought of the grimace that the cardinal will make; he will be furious; but I do not care, I am quite right this time."

The king bowed to M. de Tréville and the latter joined his musketeers, whom he found sharing the forty pistoles which his Majesty had given d'Artagnan.

The cardinal was in reality as furious as his master had anticipated—so furious, in fact, that for eight days he took no hand at the king's card-table. But this did not prevent the king from putting on the most charming face, and asking every time he met him, in a most insinuating tone:

"Well, M. le Cardinal! How is your poor Bernajoux? And your poor Jussac?"

3

Beginnings of an Intrigue

When d'Artagnan had left the Louvre, and had consulted his friends what he ought to do with his share of the forty pistoles, Athos advised him to order a good dinner, and Porthos to hire a lackey.

The dinner was accomplished on the same day; and the lackey waited at table. The dinner had been ordered by Athos; and the lackey, who had been provided by Porthos, was a Picard, by the name of Planchet.

Porthos's own lackey was called Mousqueton. Athos had a valet, whom he had drilled to his service in a manner peculiar to himself, and whose name was Grimaud. He was very taciturn, this worthy signor—we mean Athos, not his man. He had accustomed Grimaud to obey him at a simple gesture or at the mere movement of his lips. He never spoke to him except on the most extraordinary occasions. Aramis had a servant called Bazin who, thanks to the hopes which his master entertained of some day taking orders, always dressed in black, as became a churchman's servant.

Now that we know, at least superficially, the masters and the men, let us turn to their habitations

Athos dwelt in the Rue Férou, at two steps from the Luxembourg. His lodging consisted of two small rooms in a very neatly furnished house, whose mistress was still young and pretty, but ogled him in vain. Some few fragments of long-departed splendour adorned the walls of this modest lodging; such as a richly mounted sword, which looked of the age of Francis I, and of which the handle alone encrusted with precious stones, might be worth about two hundred pistoles. Nevertheless, Athos, even in moments of the greatest distress, could never be persuaded to dispose of it or to pawn it. This sword had long excited the envy of Porthos, who would willingly have given ten years of his life for the possession of it.

Porthos inhabited a lodging of vast size, and of most sumptuous appearance, in the Rue du Vieux Colombier Every time Porthos passed the windows of his house, at one of which Mousqueton was sure to be standing in splendid livery, he raised his head and hand saying: "Behold my habitation!" But no one ever found him at home, nor did he ever ask anyone in, and it was therefore impossible to form an idea of the reality of those riches which this sumptuous appearance promised.

As for Aramis, he dwelt in a small apartment in the Rue de Vaugirard, comprising a drawing-room, a dining-room, and a bedroom, which were on the ground floor, and had access to a small garden, fresh, green, shady, and quite impenetrable to the eyes of the surrounding neighbourhood.

D'Artagnan, who was naturally very curious, as men of talent generally are, made every effort to find out who Athos, Porthos and Aramis really were; for, under one of those assumed appellations each of these young men concealed his real name. However, he did not succeed.

The days of the four young men passed happily on. Athos played, and always with ill-luck, yet he never borrowed a sou of his friends, although he lent to them when he could. And when he played on credit, he always awoke his creditor at six in the morning to pay him the debt of the evening before. Porthos had his humours; one day, if he gained, he was insolent and splendid; and when he lost, he disappeared entirely for a time, and then came back, wan and thin, but with his pockets stored with coin. As for Aramis, he never played; he was the worst musketeer and the most unconvivial guest possible. He always had something to do. Even in the middle of dinner, when all expected him to spend two or three hours enjoying the wine and company, out came his watch, and he would say, rising with a graceful smile, and taking leave of the company, that he must consult a casuist with whom he had an appointment. He was a young fellow made up of mysteries, who eluded all questions concerning himself.

Planchet, d'Artagnan's valet, nobly supported his good fortune. He received thirty sous a day; and, for a whole month, entered the lodgings gay as a chaffinch, and affable to his master. When the wind of adversity began to blow on the household of the Rue des Fossoyeurs—that is to say, when King Louis XIII's forty pistoles were eaten up, or nearly so—he began to utter complaints which Athos found very nauseous, Porthos indelicate and Aramis ridiculous. So d'Artagnan, on the advice of Porthos, thrashed his lackey and Planchet, seized with admiration for his master's manner of acting, said no more about going away.

The lives of the four young men were now passed alike. D'Artagnan, who had formed no habits whatever, as he had but just arrived from the provinces and fallen into the midst of a world entirely new to him, immediately assumed those of his friends.

They rose at eight in the winter and six in the summer; and went to take the countersign and see what was doing at M. de Tréville's. D'Artagnan, though he was not a musketeer, performed the duties of one with touching punctuality. He was always on guard, as he always accompanied that one of his friends whose turn it chanced to be

In the meantime, the promises of M. de Tréville were fulfilled. One fine day, the king commanded the Chevalier des Essarts to take d'Artagnan as a recruit into his company of guards. It was not without a sigh that d'Artagnan put on the uniform, which he would have exchanged for that of the musketeers at the cost of ten years of his existence. But M. de Tréville had promised him that favour after a cadetship of two years; a cadetship which, however, might be abridged, if he should find an opportunity of distinguishing himself by some brilliant action. D'Artagnan retired with this promise, and entered on his service the next day.

Then it was that Athos, Porthos and Aramis mounted guard in turn with d'Artagnan, when he was on duty. The company of M. des Essarts, therefore, on the day that it received the youthful Gascon, received four men in the place of one!

Alas, the fortunes of our four companions fell to a low ebb. As the funds of one were exhausted, the others came to the rescue. They began to depend increasingly on invitations to obtain meals. One day, when in this parlous financial plight, there was a knock on d'Artagnan's door. A man of plain and simple appearance, who had the air of a tradesman, was introduced

"I have heard M. d'Artagnan mentioned as a very brave young man," said this citizen, "and this it is that has determined me to confide a secret to him. I have a wife who is seamstress to the queen, and who is not without wit or beauty. I was induced to marry her three years ago, though she had but a small dowry, because M. de la Porte, the queen's cloak-bearer, is her godfather and patron."

"Well, sir?" demanded d'Artagnan.

"Well, sir," replied the citizen, "she was abducted yesterday morning as she left her workroom."

"And by whom has she been carried off?" inquired d'Artagnan.

"I do not know positively, sir," said the other; "but I suspect a certain person."

"And who is this person whom you suspect?"

"One who has for a long time pursued her."

"The deuce he has!"

"But allow me to tell you, sir, that there is less of love than policy in all this. I believe it is in consequence of no love affair of her own that my wife has been entrapped, but because of an amour of a lady of far more exalted station than her own."

"Ah, ah! Can it be on account of some amour of Madame de Bois-Tracy?"

"Higher, sir, higher!"

"Of Madame d'Aiguillon?"

"Higher yet!"

"Of Madame de Chevreuse?"

"Higher, sir, higher!"

"Of the—"

And here d'Artagnan paused.

"Yes!" answered the frightened citizen, in such a low voice as to be scarcely audible.

"And who is the other party?" asked d'Artagnan, after assuring the man he would keep the secret.

"Who can it be, if not the Duke of—" replied the citizen after a long pause.

"But how do you know all this?"

"I know it from my wife, sir—from my wife herself."

"And from whom does she know it?"

"From M. de la Porte. Did I not tell you that she is his god-daughter? Well, M. de la Porte, who is the confidential agent of the queen, had placed her near her Majesty, so that the poor thing—abandoned as she is by the king, watched as she is by the cardinal, and betrayed as she is by all—might at any rate have someone in whom she could confide."

"Ah, ah! I begin to understand," said d'Artagnan.

"Now, sir, my wife came home four days ago. One of the conditions of our marriage was that she should come and see me twice a week; for, as I have the honour to inform you, sir, she loves me dearly. Well, sir, she came to inform me, in confidence, that the queen is at the present time in great alarm."

"Really?" said d'Artagnan.

"Yes! The cardinal, as it appears, spies upon her and persecutes her more than ever; he cannot pardon her the episode of the sarabande—you know the story of the sarabande, sir?"

"Egad! I should think I do!" replied d'Artagnan; who knew nothing at all about it, but would not for the world appear ignorant.

"So that it is no longer hatred now, but revenge!" said the citizen.

"Really!" replied d'Artagnan.

"And the queen believes—"

"Well! What does the queen believe?"

"She believes that they have forged a letter in her name to the Duke of Buckingham."

"In her Majesty's name?"

"Yes, to entice him to Paris; and when they have got him here, to lead him into some snare."

"The deuce! But your wife, my dear sir—what is her part in all this?"

"They know her devotion to the queen, and want to separate her from her mistress; and either to intimidate her into betraying her Majesty's secrets, or seduce her into serving as a spy upon her."

"Do you know her abductor?" said d'Artagnan. "Do you know him by sight?"

"Yes, my wife pointed him out one day."

"Has he any mark by which he may be recognized?"

"Yes, certainly; he is a man of aristocratic appearance, and has black hair, a swarthy complexion, piercing eyes, white teeth, and a scar on his forehead."

"A scar on his forehead!" cried d'Artagnan; "and with white teeth, piercing eyes, dark complexion, and proud air—it is my man of Meung!"

"Your man, do you say?"

"Yes, yes!" said d'Artagnan;"but this has nothing to do with this. No, I am mistaken! It has on the contrary, a great deal to do with it; for if your man is mine also, I shall at one blow perform two acts of revenge. But where can I meet him?"

"I have not the slightest idea. One day when I was accompanying my wife back to the Louvre, he came out as she entered, and she pointed him out to me."

"Plague on it!" murmured d'Artagnan. "This is all very vague. But how did you hear of your wife's abduction?"

"From M. de la Porte."

"Did he tell you the details?"

"He knew none."

"You have got no information from other quarters?"

"Yes, I have received—"

"You return to your hesitation; but permit me to observe that you have now advanced too far to retreat."

"I do not draw back," exclaimed the citizen, accompanying the assurance with an oath, to keep his courage up; "besides, on the honour of Bonacieux—"

"Then your name is Bonacieux?" interrupted d'Artagnan.

"Yes, that is my name."

"Pardon this interruption, but the name appears familiar to me."

"It is very possible, sir, for I am your landlord."

"Ah, ah!" said d'Artagnan, half rising. "Ah, you are my landlord?"

"Yes, sir, yes; and as for the three months you have been in my house (diverted, no doubt, by your great and splendid occupations) you have forgotten to pay me my rent, and as, likewise, I have not once asked you for payment, I thought that you would have some regard for my delicacy in that respect."

"Why, I have no alternative, my dear M. Bonacieux," answered d'Artagnan, "believe me, I am grateful for such conduct; finish what you were about to say."

Bonacieux drew a paper from his pocket and gave it to d'Artagnan.

"A letter!" exclaimed the young man.

"Which I received this morning."

D'Artagnan opened it, and, as the light had commenced to wane, he went to the window, followed by Bonacieux.

" "Do not seek for your wife," " read d'Artagnan; " "she will be restored to you when she is no longer required. If you make a single attempt to discover her, you are lost!" Well, this is pretty positive," he continued, "but after all, it is only a threat."

"Yes, but this threat frightens me, sir; I am not at all warlike, and I fear the Bastille."

"Humph!" said d'Artagnan. "I do not like the Bastille any more than you do; if it was only a sword-thrust, now, it would be of no consequence."

Bonacieux was going on to appeal afresh to d'Artagnan for help, when he stopped in mid-sentence. "Whom do I see yonder?" he cried suddenly.

"Where?"

"In the street, opposite; in the opening of that entry—a man wrapped in a cloak!"

"It is he!" cried d'Artagnan and Bonacieux in one breath, each at the same time having recognized his man.

"Ah! This time he shall not escape me!" exclaimed d'Artagnan rushing out, sword in hand.

On the staircase he met Athos and Porthos, who were coming to see him. They stood apart and he passed between them like an arrow.

"Ah, where are you off to?" cried the two musketeers.

"The man of Meung!" ejaculated d'Artagnan, as he disappeared.

When they entered the room which d'Artagnan had just quitted, they found it empty; for the landlord, fearing the consequences of the meeting and duel which he felt certain was about to take place between the young man and the stranger, had judged it most prudent to decamp.

Athos and Porthos guessed that after overtaking his man or losing sight of him d'Artagnan would return. He again missed his man, and in half an hour came back to his lodgings. Meanwhile, Aramis had joined his companions, so that on his return d'Artagnan found the reunion complete.

"Well?" exclaimed they, when they saw him enter, covered with perspiration, and furious.

"Well!" said he, throwing his sword on the bed; "this man must be the devil himself; he disappeared like a phantom, a shadow, a spectre! His escape has caused us to miss a fine opportunity—one, gentlemen, by which a hundred pistoles or more were to be gained! Planchet, go to my landlord, M. Bonacieux, and tell him to send me half a dozen bottles of Beaugency, which is my favourite wine."

He then related, word for word, all that had passed between him and his landlord; and how the man who had carried off the worthy citizen's wife, was the same with whom he had quarrelled at the Jolly Miller, at Meung. "And I am convinced," concluded d'Artagnan, "that the abduction of this woman, one of the queen's suite, has some connection with the cardinal's persecution of the queen, and perhaps with the presence of the Englishman, the Duke of Buckingham, in Paris."

"Gentlemen," said Aramis, "listen!"

"Let us listen to Aramis!" exclaimed the three friends.

"Yesterday I was at the house of a learned doctor of theology whom I sometimes consult about my studies. He has a niece who comes sometimes to see her uncle, and as she was there by chance at the same time that I was, I was obliged to offer to conduct her to her carriage. All of a sudden a tall dark man, with the manners of a gentleman—like your man, d'Artagnan—"

"The same, perhaps," said the Gascon.

"It is possible," said Aramis. "He approached me, accompanied by five or six men, who followed him at about ten paces, and in the politest tone said, "My lord Duke, and you, Madame," addressing the lady, "be so kind as to enter that carriage, without resistance, and in silence.""

"He took you for Buckingham?" said d'Artagnan.

"Almost certainly," said Aramis.

"But this lady?" said Porthos.

"He took her for the queen," said d'Artagnan.

"Precisely!" said Aramis.

"The Gascon is the devil," said Athos; "nothing escapes him!"

"The fact is," said Porthos, "that Aramis is about the height, and has something of the figure, of the handsome duke; and yet one would think that the uniform of a musketeer—"

"I had on an enormous cloak."

"In the month of July! Excellent!" cried Porthos. "Was the doctor afraid that you might be recognized?"

"I can conceive," said Athos, "that the spy might be deceived by your figure; but your face?"

"I had a large hat on," replied Aramis.

"What extraordinary precautions for studying theology!" exclaimed Porthos.

"Gentlemen," said d'Artagnan, "do not let us waste our time in jesting; let us rather make inquiries and search for the landlord's wife; she may prove a key to the intrigue. She is the god-daughter of La Porte, who is the confidential servant of the queen. Perhaps it is her Majesty's policy to seek assistance from a source so humble. Lofty heads are visible at a distance, and the cardinal has a good eye."

"Well then," said Porthos, "come to terms with the landlord immediately, and good terms."

"It is unnecessary," said d'Artagnan. "If he were not to pay us, we shall be well enough paid from another quarter."

At this moment, a noise of hasty steps was heard upon the stairs; the door opened with a crash, and the unhappy Bonacieux rushed into the room in which this council was being held. "Oh, gentlemen," he exclaimed, "save me, save me! In the name of heaven save me! There are four men come to arrest me!"

Porthos and Aramis rose.

"One moment," cried d'Artagnan, making them a sign to sheath their swords, which they had half-drawn, "wait a moment! It is not courage, but diplomacy, that we need here!"

"Nevertheless," said Porthos, "we will not permit—"

"Give d'Artagnan a free hand," said Athos; "he is the cleverest of the party, and, for my part, I declare that I will obey him. Do what you like, d'Artagnan."

As this speech was uttered the four guards appeared at the door of the anteroom, but seeing four musketeers standing there, with swords at their sides, they hesitated to advance any further.

Yet d'Artagnan, despite protests from his landlord, permitted his arrest and even drank the health of the leader of the guards. Athos and Aramis congratulated him on his subtlety, though Porthos was puzzled by these actions

"Now", said d'Artagnan, "attention! From this moment we are at war with the Cardinal."

Everyone who now came into or left the house of M. Bonacieux was questioned by the police, who established themselves permanently there. Arrests were kept secret and by this method soon they had in their power all the frequenters of the establishment. The officers at the Bonacieux home were the cardinal's men, but owing to d'Artagnan's cordiality his own visitors were not molested. He had made a hole in the floor of the room above that where the questioning took place, and stayed in all the time to listen to what was said below. He expected to hear the questions, "Is the Duke of Buckingham in Paris and has he had an interview with the queen?" but he heard little of interest until someone was brought in bound. It proved to be Madame Bonacieux herself. Cries and moans and the sound of struggles followed. Hastily telling Planchet to fetch his three friends, d'Artagnan dropped from the first floor window to the ground, knocked at the door, entered, sword in hand, and after a short struggle sent the four men clothed in black whom he found in the room, only one of whom was armed, flying out of the house.

When d'Artagnan was left alone with Madame Bonacieux, he found the poor woman had fallen back on an armchair, almost senseless. D'Artagnan examined her with a rapid glance.

She was a charming woman of about twenty-five or twenty-six years of age, with dark hair, blue eyes, a nose slightly turned up, beautiful teeth and a complexion of intermingled rose and opal. Here, however, ended the charms which might have confounded her with a lady of high birth. Her hands were white but not delicately formed, and her feet did not indicate a woman of quality. Fortunately, d'Artagnan was not of an age to be nice in these matters.

On the ground he noticed a fine cambric handkerchief, which, naturally, he picked up, and at the corner of it he discovered the same cipher that he had seen on the handkerchief which had nearly caused him and Aramis to cut one another's throats. Since that time d'Artagnan had mistrusted all coroneted handkerchiefs; so he now put the one he had picked up into Madame Bonacieux's pocket, without saying a word. At that moment Madame Bonacieux recovered her senses. She immediately held out her hands to him with a smile—and Madame Bonacieux had the most charming smile in the world.

"Ah, sir," said she, "it is you who have saved me; allow me to thank you."

"Madame," replied d'Artagnan, "I have only done what any gentleman would have done in my place. You owe me no thanks."

"What did these men, whom I first took for robbers, want with me? And why is M. Bonacieux not here?"

"Madame, these men were far more dangerous than any robbers would have been, for they are agents of the cardinal; and as for your husband, M. Bonacieux, he is not here because he was taken yesterday to the Bastille."

"My husband in the Bastille!" cried Madame Bonacieux. Oh, my God! What can he have done, poor, dear man! Why, he is innocence itself!"

"I believe," replied d'Artagnan, "that his only crime consists in having at the same time the good fortune and the misfortune of being your husband."

"Then, sir, you know?"

"I know that you were carried off, Madame, by a man about forty or forty-five years of age, with dark hair, a smart complexion, and a scar on the left temple. But I don't know his name. Your husband knew you had been carried off but suspected that it was for a political motive."

A smile, almost imperceptible, glided over the rosy lips of the beautiful young woman.

"But," continued d'Artagnan, "how did you escape?"

"I profited by a moment in which I was left alone; and as I learned this morning the reason for my abduction, I got out of the window by the help of my sheets, and hurried here, where I expected to find my husband."

"To place yourself under his protection?"

"Oh, no, poor, dear man! I knew that he was incapable of protecting me; but as he might be of some service to us, I wished to put him on his guard."

"Against what?"

"Alas! That is not my secret; and I dare not tell it to you."

D'Artagnan and Madame Bonacieux now planned to escape from the house and inform M. de la Porte at the Louvre of what had happened. So leaving Madame Bonacieux at Athos's house, which was empty, d'Artagnan, armed by her with the password, entered the Louvre and told M. de la Porte what was going on, and where Madame Bonacieux was to be found. La Porte made certain of the address by having it twice repeated, and then hurried away. But he had scarcely taken ten steps before he returned.

"Young man," he said, "let me give you some good counsel."

"What is it?"

"You may possibly get into some trouble from this affair."

"Do you think so?"

"Have you any friend whose clock is slow?"

"Suppose I have?"

"Go and pay him a visit that he may be able to bear witness that you were in his company at half-past nine. In law, that is what is called an alibi."

D'Artagnan thought the advice prudent. He therefore visited M. de Tréville, and while alone in his office, moved the hands of his clock back. After a long story of the intrigue, during which he induced M. de Tréville to look at the time, he left, but on the excuse of having forgotten his cane, he returned to M. de Tréville's office and hastily put the clock right once more. Meanwhile, his heart beat fast at the thought of pretty Madame Bonacieux. That she was rich did not escape the thoughts of d'Artagnan. Her mercer husband had confessed to him that he was rich, and it was easy to infer that, with a simpleton like Bonacieux, the wife would be the keeper of the purse. In those days men did not blush at owing their advancement to women.

4

Important Persons are Involved

Finding himself in Aramis's neighbourhood, d'Artagnan thought he might as well pay him a visit, to explain why he had sent Planchet with the invitation to come immediately to his lodging. He realized that if Planchet had found Aramis at home, the latter had probably hastened to the Rue des Fossoyeurs, and finding nobody there but Athos and Porthos, they would have all been in ignorance of what the summons meant. This needed some explanation; or, at least, so said d'Artagnan aloud.

But, in his inner soul, he thought that this call would give him an opportunity of talking of the pretty Madame Bonacieux, with whom his mind, if not his heart, was already quite occupied. It is not in a first love that we must look for discretion. The joy with which such a love is attended is so exuberant, that it must overflow or it would suffocate us.

For the last two hours Paris had been dark and nearly deserted. Eleven o'clock was striking from all the clocks of the Faubourg St. Germain, and the weather was mild.

D'Artagnan had already just perceived the door of his friend's house in the Rue de Vaugirard, shaded by sycamores and clematis, when he saw something like a shadow which came out of the Rue Servandoni. This something was enveloped in a cloak, and d'Artagnan thought at first that it was a man; but from the smallness of its size, the irresolution of its manner, and its impeded step, he soon became convinced that it must be a woman. And, moreover, this woman, as though she was uncertain of the house she sought for, lifted up her eyes to examine, stopped, turned back, and then retraced her steps. D'Artagnan was at a loss.

Suppose I should go and proffer my services!" thought he. Then he suddenly remembered the theologian's niece. "It would be droll," he said to himself, "if this wandering dove is looking for my friend's house. But, upon my soul, it seems very probable. Ah, my dear Aramis! I will find out about it once and for all."

Making himself as small as possible, d'Artagnan concealed himself in the most obscure part of the street, near a stone bench placed at the back of a niche.

The young woman continued to advance; for besides the lightness of her step which had betrayed her, she had just given a slight small cough which denoted a gentle voice. D'Artagnan believed this cough was a signal. The lady knocked resolutely three times, at equal intervals, with her bent finger, on the shutter of Aramis's window.

"It is really Aramis's house," muttered d'Artagnan. "Ah, Mr. Hypocrite, is this how you study theology?"

Scarcely had the three taps been given, before the inner casement opened and a light appeared.

"Ah, ah!" said the listener. "Not at the door, but the window! Ah, ah! The visit was expected. Come, the shutter will be opened presently and the lady will get in by escalade. Pretty!"

But, to his great astonishment, the shutter continued closed; and what was more, the light which had flashed for an instant, disappeared, and all became dark again.

D'Artagnan thought that this could not last, and continued to watch. He was right; in a few seconds two knocks were heard from inside; and when the young woman in the street answered by one knock, the shutter opened.

D'Artagnan saw the young woman take from her pocket something white, which she unfolded quickly and which looked like a pocket handkerchief, and she then drew the attention of the person she addressed to the corner of the object she unfolded.

This reminded d'Artagnan of the handkerchief he had found at Madame Bonacieux's feet which also had recalled to his mind the one that he had pulled from under Aramis's foot.

What the deuce, then, could this handkerchief mean?

Placed where he was, d'Artagnan could not see Aramis's face—we say Aramis, because he had no doubt that it was his friend who was conversing from the inside with the lady outside. His curiosity, therefore, overcame his prudence; and profiting by the earnest attention which the sight of the handkerchief excited in the two persons whom we have described, he left his place of concealment and, quickly as lightning, yet with cautious step, placed himself near a corner of the wall from which his eye could completely overlook the inside of Aramis's apartment.

On reaching this spot he was scarcely able to restrain an exclamation of surprise. It was not Aramis who was conferring with the midnight visitor, but a woman. At that moment the woman in the room drew a handkerchief from her own pocket, and exchanged it for the one which had been shown to her. A few words were then pronounced by the two women, the shutter was closed, and the woman in the street turned, and, lowering the hood of her cloak, passed within four paces of d'Artagnan. But her precaution had been taken too late; he had already recognized Madame Bonacieux.

Curious to find out more and tormented by pangs of jealousy, d'Artagnan ran after her. It was no great difficulty for him to catch a woman encumbered by a large cloak. He overtook her, in fact, before she had gone a third of the street. The poor woman was exhausted, not by fatigue, but by terror; and when d'Artagnan put his hand upon her shoulder, she sank upon one knee, exclaiming in a suffocated voice:

"Kill me if you will; you shall learn nothing!"

D'Artagnan raised her up and she opened her eyes, cast one glance upon the man who had so frightened her, and seeing that it was d'Artagnan, gave utterance to a cry of joy.

"Oh! It is you, it is you," said she. "God be thanked!"

"Yes; it is I," said d'Artagnan, "whom God has sent to guard you."

"And was it with this intention that you followed me?" asked the young woman, with a smile full of coquetry; for all her fears had vanished.

"No," replied d'Artagnan, "no, I confess that it is chance which put me on your track. I saw a woman knocking at the window of one of my friends—Aramis."

"Aramis! Who is he?"

"Come, now, you are not going to tell me that you do not know Aramis?"

"Most assuredly I do not! Besides, you must have plainly seen that the person whom I talked to was a woman."

"That is true; but then this woman may be one of Aramis's friends! Who is she?"

"That is not my secret."

"My dear Madame Bonacieux, you are very charming, but you are at the same time the most mysterious creature. It lends you enchantment!"

"As that is the case, give me your arm."

"With great pleasure; what now?"

"Now take me with you."

"Where to?"

"You will see, since you will leave me at the door."

"May I wait for you there?"

"That would be useless."

"Then you will return alone?"

"Possibly."

But Madame Bonacieux was firm. She made d'Artagnan promise on his word as a gentleman not to wait and see with whom she came out. "Take my arm, and let us go on," she finished.

D'Artagnan offered his arm, which Madame Bonacieux, half laughing, and half trembling, accepted, and they reached the top of the Rue de la Harpe; but the young woman appeared to hesitate there, as she had hesitated before at the Rue de Vaugirard. Nevertheless, by certain marks, she appeared to recognize a door, which she approached.

"Now, sir," said she, "it is here that my business calls me. I return you a thousand thanks for your good company, which has saved me from all the dangers to which I should have been exposed alone; but the time is now come for you to keep your word. You must leave me here."

"And will you be exposed to no danger in returning?"

"I shall only have to fear robbers."

"Is that nothing?"

"What could they take from me? I have not a farthing in my possession!

"You forget that beautiful embroidered handkerchief, with the arms on it, which a found at your feet, and replaced in your pocket."

"Silence! Silence! You imprudent man! Would you ruin me?"

"But you, Madame, prudent as you are, think, if you were to be arrested with that handkerchief on you, could you not be compromised?"

"In what way? Are not the initials mine? C.B.—Constance Bonacieux."

"Or Camille de Bois-Tracy."

"Silence, sir! In the name of Heaven, depart!"

She refused to answer any more questions and when d'Artagnan declared his love for her replied she as yet felt no more than gratitude to him, whatever she might feel in the future. Eventually he realized she was becoming impatient, so he released her hand, and hastily ran off, whilst Madame Bonacieux rapped three times at the door, slowly and regularly, as she had done at the window shutter.

At the corner of the street he turned, but the door had been opened and closed again, and his landlord's pretty wife had disappeared.

D'Artagnan proceeded on his way. He had promised Madame

Bonacieux not to watch her; and, had his life depended on a knowledge of the place that she was going to, or the person who went with her, he would still have gone home, as he had promised to do. In five minutes he was in the Rue des Fossoyeurs.

"Poor Athos!" said he. "He will not understand all this. He will have fallen asleep waiting for me, or he will have returned home, and will have learned that there has been a woman there. A woman at *his* house! After all," continued d'Artagnan, "there certainly was one at Aramis's. All this is very strange, and I shall be extremely curious to know how it will end."

When he got home Planchet informed him that Athos had been arrested by the guard brought by the men in black, whom d'Artagnan had put to flight. Athos had been mistaken for d'Artagnan, but had been careful not to give his name, in order to allow d'Artagnan his liberty. Planchet had been unable to find Porthos and Aramis.

Telling Planchet not to stir from there, d'Artagnan ran towards M. de Tréville's house in the Rue du Colombier as fast as his legs could carry him.

M. de Tréville was not at home. His company was on guard at the Louvre; and he was at the Louvre with it.

It was necessary, however, to see M. de Tréville; it was important that he should be informed of these events. D'Artagnan therefore determined to obtain an entrance to the Louvre. His uniform, as one of M. des Essarts' guards ought to be a passport for admission.

When he reached the riverside, he saw two persons, a man and a woman, whose appearance struck him, coming out of the Rue Dauphine. The woman resembled Madame Bonacieux and the man was so like Aramis that he might be mistaken for him. Besides, the woman had on the black cloak which d'Artagnan could still imagine outlined on the shutter in the Rue de Vaugirard and on the door in the Rue de la Harpe. Moreover, the man wore the uniform of the musketeers.

The woman's hood was pulled down and the man held his handkerchief in front of his face. This double precaution showed that they were both anxious to escape recognition.

They went over the bridge, and this was also d'Artagnan's road as he was going to the Louvre; he therefore followed them. Scarcely, however, had he taken twenty steps before he was convinced that the woman was Madame Bonacieux and the man Aramis.

At that very instant he felt fermenting in his heart all the suspicious torments of jealousy. He was doubly betrayed, betrayed both by his friend, and by her whom he had already loved as a mistress.

D'Artagnan hastened on, passed them, then turned and stopped in front of them by a lamp on the bridge; and they stopped also.

"What do you want, sir?" asked the musketeer, recoiling a step, and in a foreign accent which proved to d'Artagnan that he was at least deceived in one of his conjectures.

"It is not Aramis!" exclaimed d'Artagnan.

"No, sir, it is not Aramis; and as I find by your exclamation that you mistook me for another, I excuse you."

"Excuse me, indeed!" exclaimed d'Artagnan.

"Yes," replied the unknown; "now let me pass on, since it is not with me that you have anything to do."

But now d'Artagnan was reproached by Madame Bonacieux for interfering. "I thought I could depend on the promise of a soldier and the word of a gentleman," she said.

Stunned, overwhelmed, annihilated by all that had happened— he remained standing, with his arms crossed, before the musketeer and Madame Bonacieux.

The former came forward two paces and pushed d'Artagnan aside with his hand.

D'Artagnan made one bound backwards and drew his sword. At the same moment, and with the quickness of lightning, the stranger drew his.

"In God's name, my lord!" cried Madame Bonacieux, throwing herself between the combatants, and seizing their swords with both her hands.

"My lord!" cried d'Artagnan, enlightened by a sudden idea. "My lord, pardon me, sir, but can you be—"

"My Lord Duke of Buckingham!" said Madame Bonacieux in a very low voice. "And now you may destroy us all."

"My lord—Madame—pardon me; a thousand pardons; but, my lord, I love her and was jealous. You know, my lord, what it is to love! Pardon me, and tell me how I may die in your Grace's cause."

"You are a brave youth," said Buckingham, offering him a hand, which d'Artagnan pressed respectfully. "You offer me your services and I accept them. Follow us, at the distance of twenty paces, to the Louvre, and if anyone dogs our steps, kill him!"

D'Artagnan put his naked sword under his arm, let the duke and Madame Bonacieux go forward about twenty steps, and then followed them, ready to execute to the letter the instructions of the elegant and noble minister of Charles I.

But, fortunately, the young volunteer had no opportunity of affording this proof of his devotion to the duke; and the young woman and the handsome musketeer entered the Louvre by the wicket gate without any interference.

As for d'Artagnan, he went immediately to the Pineapple Tavern, where he found Porthos and Aramis waiting for him. But without giving them any further reason for the trouble he had caused them, he told them that he had himself concluded the business for which he had at first thought he would have wanted their assistance.

And now, let us follow, amidst the tortuous corridors of the Louvre, the Duke of Buckingham and his guide.

Madame Bonacieux and the duke entered the Louvre without any difficulty; Madame Bonacieux was known to be of the queen's household; and the duke wore the uniform of the musketeers of M. de Tréville, who, as we have said, were on guard that evening.

Once inside the court, the duke and the young woman kept close to the wall for about twenty-five paces; at the end of which Madame Bonacieux tried a small side-door which was usually open during the day, but closed at night. The door opened and they both entered, and found themselves in total darkness; but Madame Bonacieux was well acquainted with all the turnings and twistings of this part of the Louvre, which was set apart for persons of the royal suite. After many passages and stairs had been traversed she pushed her companion into a room lighted only by a night-lamp, saying to him: "Remain here, my lord duke; someone will come immediately." Then she went out by the same door, locking it after her, so that the duke found himself literally a prisoner

Yet though thus deserted, as it were, he did not feel the slightest fear. George Villiers, Duke of Buckingham, had engaged in one of those fabled existences which remain, throughout the course of centuries, an astonishment to posterity.

Placing himself before a glass, the duke rearranged his beautiful fair hair, of which the pressure of his hat had disordered the curls, and twisted his moustache; and then, his heart swelling with joy, happy and elated at having reached the moment he had so long desired, he smiled to himself proudly and hopefully.

At that moment a door concealed in the tapestry opened, and a woman entered. Buckingham saw the reflection in the glass; he uttered a cry; it was the queen!

Anne of Austria was at that time twenty-six or twenty-seven years of age—that is, she was in all the glory of her beauty. Her deportment was that of a queen, or a goddess Her eyes, which shone like emeralds, were perfectly beautiful; but at the same time full of gentleness and majesty. Her mouth was small and rosy; and though her under-lip, like that of the princes of the house of Austria, protruded slightly beyond the other, her smile was eminently gracious, but at the same time could be profoundly haughty in its scorn. Her skin was celebrated for its velvet softness, and her hand and arm were of such surpassing beauty as to be immortalized as incomparable by all the poets of the time. Admirably, too, did her hair, which in her youth had been fair, but had now become chestnut, and which she wore plainly dressed, and with much powder, shade a face on which the most rigid critic could have desired only a little less rouge, and the most fastidious sculptor only a little more delicacy in the formation of the nose.

Buckingham remained an instant perfectly dazzled. Anne of Austria had never appeared to him so beautiful even in the midst of balls and festivals and entertainments, as she now appeared in her simple robe of white satin, and accompanied by Donna Estefana, the only one of her Spanish ladies who had not been driven from her by the jealousy of the king and the persecutions of the cardinal.

Anne of Austria advanced two steps; the duke threw himself at her feet, and before the queen could prevent him, had kissed the hem of her robe.

"My lord, you already know that it was not I who sent for you from England?"

"Oh yes, madame! Yes, your Majesty!" exclaimed Buckingham. "I know that I have been a fool, a madman, to believe that the snow could have been animated, that the marble could grow warm; but what would you expect? The lover easily believes in love; nor has my journey been entirely in vain, since I behold you now."

Anne then reproved him for his folly in remaining in Paris but she was flattered by Buckingham's eager description of her as she was at their last meeting. He declared his love for her with such passion that Anne's heart was touched. Buckingham told her that, although he could not now be allowed to see her again, she would hear him spoken of when he attacked France. The war might bring about a peace; he would be the negotiator for that peace. He would again be in her adopted country, and would see her, and be happy for an instant.

Anne of Austria returned to her apartment, and came back almost immediately, holding in her hand a small casket of rosewood, with her monogram encrusted in gold. "Here, my lord, here! Keep this as a memorial of me!"

Buckingham took the casket and again sank upon his knee, then true to the promise he had given her, to leave France, he rushed out of the room.

In the corridor he found Madame Bonacieux awaiting him; and with the same precaution, and the same good fortune, she led him out of the Louvre.

Now we must turn our attention to the fortunes of M. Bonacieux.

The officers who had arrested him, conducted him at once to the Bastille, where he had to pass, trembling, before a company of soldiers, who were charging their muskets. Taken from there into a half-subterranean gallery, he had to endure the most brutal insults and harsh treatment The jailers saw that he was not a nobleman, and they therefore treated him like a beggar.

In about half an hour, a registrar came to put an end to his tortures, but not to his anxiety, by ordering that he should be conducted to the examination chamber.

The superintendent of police was a man with a sharp nose; cheeks yellow and puffed out; small, but piercing eyes; and an expression reminding one, at the same time, of a polecat and a fox. His head, supported by a long and flexible neck, was thrust out of his full black robe, and balanced itself with a motion very much like that of a turtle putting its head out of a shell.

He began by asking M. Bonacieux his full name, his age, profession and place of abode.

The accused replied that his name was Jacques Bonacieux, that he was 51 years old, that he was a retired mercer, and lived at No. 11 Rue des Fossoyeurs.

Instead of continuing his questions, the superintendent then made a long speech on the danger of an obscure citizen interfering in public affairs. With this exordium he combined an exposition of the power and actions of the cardinal—that incomparable minister, the conqueror of all preceding ministers, and the example for all future ministers—whom no one could oppose or thwart with impunity.

After this second part of his discourse, he fixed his hawk's eye on poor Bonacieux, and exhorted him to reflect upon the seriousness of his position.

This the mercer had already done; he consigned M. de la Porte to the devil for ever putting it into his head to marry his goddaughter, and cursed the hour when that god-daughter had been received into the queen's service.

The character of M. Bonacieux was one of profound selfishness, mingled with sordid avarice, the whole being seasoned with excessive cowardice. The love which he entertained towards his young wife was quite a secondary sentiment, and could not stand against those primary feelings which we have just enumerated.

He disclaimed all accusations of treason and hastened to tell the superintendent all about his wife's abduction and the man who abducted her. He did not know the man's name, but said he would recognize him among a thousand. This admission caused the superintendent's face to grow still darker and he ordered Bonacieux to be cast into the safest dungeon. Then he hastily wrote a letter putting down all the facts Bonacieux had told him.

Poor Bonacieux could not close his eyes; not because his dungeon was very uncomfortable, but because his anxiety was too great. He sat upon his stool the whole night, trembling at every noise.

Suddenly he heard the bolts withdrawn and gave a terrible start. He believed they were coming to conduct him to the scaffold; and, therefore, when he saw it was only the superintendent and his attendant, he was almost ready to embrace them.

"Your affair has become sadly complicated since last evening, my fine fellow," said the superintendent. "I advise you to tell the whole truth, for your repentance alone can mitigate the anger of the cardinal."

The superintendent then announced that Madame Bonacieux had escaped at five o'clock the previous afternoon. And why had

M. Bonacieux appealed to d'Artagnan? On Bonacieux replying that he had asked him to help to find his wife, the superintendent sent off guards to arrest d'Artagnan, but it was Athos whom the guards led in, thinking he was d'Artagnan. At first the superintendent refused to believe he was not d'Artagnan but at last he was persuaded by Athos's uniform—that of M. de Tréville's musketeers. At that moment a letter was brought in and superintendent's attitude hardened again. Crying out that Bonacieux and his wife had arranged an infernal plan between them, he despatched Athos and Bonacieux to solitary confinement.

At nine o'clock that evening Bonacieux was taken away.

He was made to get into a carriage, was locked in with an officer by his side, and both were left in a rolling prison. He was not told where he was going, and assumed it was to be executed. He looked out through the padlocked gratings at each possible place of execution in the greatest possible terror, but each time the carriage passed on. At last it stopped, and poor Bonacieux uttered a feeble groan and fainted.

5

An Indiscreet Queen and her Problem

The carriage carrying M. Bonacieux stopped at a low doorway, and as if in a dream he found himself in an antechamber sitting on a comfortably furnished bench.

At this moment an officer of pleasant appearance opened a door, continued to exchange some words with a person in the next room, and then, turning towards the prisoner, said:

"Is your name Bonacieux?"

"Yes, sir," stammered the mercer, more dead that alive, "at your service."

"Come in!"

The officer bade the mercer precede him; and the latter, obeying without reply, entered a room where he appeared to be expected.

It was large, and its walls were furnished with offensive and defensive weapons—a close stifling room in which there was already a fire, although it was scarcely yet the end of September. A square table loaded with books and papers, on which there was unrolled an immense plan of the town of La Rochelle, occupied the middle of the apartment. In front of the fireplace there stood a man of middle height, with a proud and haughty air, piercing eyes, a large forehead, and an emaciated countenance, which was yet further elongated by an imperial, surmounted by a pair of moustaches.

Although this man was scarcely thirty-six or thirty-seven years old, both imperial and moustaches were beginning to grow grey.

His appearance, except that he wore no sword, was military; and his buff leather boots which were yet slightly covered with dust, showed that he had been on horseback during the day.

This man was Armand-Jean Duplessis, Cardinal de Richelieu.

The poor mercer remained standing at the door, whilst the eyes of the person we have been describing fixed themselves upon him as if they would penetrate his most secret thoughts.

"Is this Bonacieux?" he demanded, after a moment's pause.

"Yes, monseigneur," replied the officer.

"Very well; give me those papers and leave us."

The mercer did so, bowed to the very ground and left the room.

In these papers Bonacieux recognized his examination at the Bastille. From time to time the man by the fireplace lifted his eyes from the papers and plunged them, like daggers, into the very heart of the poor mercer.

Richelieu asked a multitude of questions but Bonacieux did not realize who was questioning him. Richelieu saw at once he was a simpleton and quite unable to carry on an intrigue. He accused him of conspiring with his wife, with Madame de Chevreuse, and the Duke of Buckingham. Bonacieux admitted hearing his wife pronounce all these names and gave Richelieu the addresses of the houses where she did business with the queen's linen-drapers, 25 Rue de Vaugirard and 75 Rue de la Harpe. On hearing these addresses Richelieu gave orders for the Count de Rochefort to be summoned.

"The count is here," said the officer, "and wishes to speak with your Eminence immediately."

"Let him come in then," said the cardinal eagerly.

"Your Eminence!" muttered Bonacieux, rolling his eyes in astonishment.

When Rochefort entered, Bonacieux cried out: "It is he—the man who took away my wife!" The cardinal rang and gave instructions for Bonacieux to be taken back to his guards.

Rochefort impatiently followed Bonacieux with his eyes till he

was gone, and as soon as the door was closed behind him, he
eagerly advanced towards the cardinal and said:

"They have met!"

"Who?" demanded the cardinal.

"Those two."

"The queen and the duke?" cried the cardinal.

"Yes."

"Where?"

"At the Louvre!"

"Are you sure?"

"Perfectly sure!"

"Who told you of it?"

"Madame de Lannoy, who is entirely devoted to your Eminence, as you know."

"Why did she not tell me sooner?"

"Either by chance or by mistrust, the queen made Madame de
Surgis sleep in her room, and kept her all day."

"Very well; we have been beaten; let us try to have our
revenge."

"Be assured that I will assist your Eminence with all my
heart."

"How did this happen?"

Rochefort then described in detail to the cardinal the meeting
between the queen and Buckingham, and told him that the casket
Anne of Austria had given the duke contained the diamond studs
which had been a present to her from the king. Thereupon Richelieu told Rochefort to ransack the houses, No. 25 Rue de Vaugirard and No. 75 Rue de la Harpe.

"It shall be done, my lord!" And Rochefort rushed from the
room.

When the cardinal was left alone he remained a moment in
thought and then ordered M. Bonacieux to be brought in again.

"You have deceived me," said the cardinal, with great severity,
when Bonacieux appeared.

"I!" cried Bonacieux. "I deceive your Eminence!"

"When your wife went to the Rue de Vaugirard, and the Rue de la Harpe, she did not go to linen-drapers."

"In God's name! Where did she go, then?"

"She went to the house of the Duchess de Chevreuse, and to the Duke of Buckingham's."

"Yes!" said Bonacieux, with a flash of recollection; "yes, exactly so; your Eminence is right. I often told my wife that it was astonishing that linen-drapers should live in such houses; in houses which had no signs; and every time I said so she began to laugh. Ah, monseigneur!" he continued, throwing himself at his Eminence's feet. "It is plain that you are the cardinal, the great cardinal—the man of genius whom all the world reveres!"

The cardinal, small as was the triumph to be achieved over so vulgar a being as Bonacieux, did not the less enjoy it for a moment. Then, as if a new idea struck him, he smiled, and, stretching out his hand to the mercer shook him by the hand, told him he was an honest man and gave him a bag containing a hundred pistoles. He told him he was free to leave and Bonacieux bowed himself out, loudly singing the praises of the cardinal.

"Here is a man who henceforward would lay down his life for me," thought the cardinal.

He then set himself to examine with great attention the map of La Rochelle, which was spread out upon the table, and to mark with a pencil the position of the famous breakwater which, eighteen months afterwards, was to close the port of the besieged city.

Whilst he was most deeply occupied with these strategic meditations, the door opened, and Rochefort reappeared.

"Well!" said the cardinal, with vivacity, which proved what consequence he attached to the intelligence he expected from the count.

"Well," said the latter, "a young woman, between twenty-six and twenty-eight years old, and a man of about thirty-five or forty years of age, have really been lodging in the houses indicated by your Eminence; but the woman left last night and the man this morning."

"It was they!" exclaimed the cardinal, whose eyes were fixed upon the clock; "but now it is too late to follow them. Madame de Chevreuse is at Tours and the duke at Boulogne. It is in London that they must be found."

"What are your Eminence's commands?"

"Let not one word be said of what has passed. Let the queen remain in perfect peace of mind; let her be ignorant that we know her secret; let her believe that we are hunting after some conspiracy. Send me Séguier, the keeper of the seals."

"And Bonacieux?"

"I have set him to spy upon his wife."

The Comte de Rochefort bowed low, like a man who felt the great superiority of his master, and withdrew.

As soon as the cardinal was again alone, he sat down once more, wrote a letter, which he sealed with his private seal and then sent for a man named Vitray.

"Vitray," said he, "you must go without an instant's delay to London, where you will give this letter to my lady. Here is a cheque for two hundred pistoles; go to my treasurer and get the money. You shall have the same sum if you return in six days, after performing my commission with success!"

The messenger, without answering one word, bowed, took the letter and the order for two hundred pistoles, and left the room.

These were the contents of the letter:

> My Lady,
> Be present at the first ball where you can meet the Duke of Buckingham. He will wear on his doublet twelve diamond studs; get close to him, and cut off two of them.
> As soon as these studs are in your possession, let me know.

On the day after these events had happened, as Athos had not returned, d'Artagnan and Porthos informed M. de Tréville of his disappearance. As for Aramis, he had requested leave of absence for five days, and it was said that he was at Rouen on some family affairs.

M. de Tréville was the father of his soldiers. The humblest individual amongst them, from the time that he put on the uniform of the company, was as certain of his assistance and support as M. de Tréville's own brother could have been.

He went, therefore, at once to the chief of police. From various inquiries it was ascertained that Athos was at that time lodged at Fort l'Evêque and had been subjected to the same trials as we have seen Bonacieux exposed to. He hastened straightway to the king.

He arrived in his Majesty's presence just after the king had learned from the lips of the cardinal that the queen had been visited by Madame de Chevreuse. The king could scarcely contain his indignation at the cardinal's news, for this friendship of Anne of Austria for Madame de Chevreuse was one of the principal causes of the king's violent prejudice against the queen, and the cardinal never lost an opportunity of fostering this prejudice. It was he who had made the king exile Madame de Chevreuse to Tours, as in his eyes she served the queen in her political and amorous intrigues. Indeed, these two women gave Richelieu more uneasiness than the war with Spain, the quarrel with England, or the embarrassment of his finances.

Because of the king's anger, M. de Tréville had a stormy interview but the king and the cardinal did not for an instant suspect Tréville's loyalty, and he affirmed positively the hour by the clock when d'Artagnan, suspected because he lodged at Bonacieux's house, had entered and left his room. At last, the king, who prided himself on being called the Just, ordered Athos, who had been mistakenly arrested, to be released.

M. de Tréville had reason to distrust the cardinal, and to think that all was not ended; for scarcely had the captain of the musketeers closed the door behind him before his Eminence said to the king:

"Now that we are alone together, we must have some serious conversation, if it please your Majesty. Sire, the Duke of Buckingham has been in Paris for five days, residing at the Rue de la Harpe, and left it only this morning."

It is impossible to form an idea of the impression which these few words produced on the king. He grew red and pale by turns, and the cardinal saw immediately that he had regained, by a single stroke, all the ground that he had previously lost.

"Buckingham in Paris!" cried the King. "What is he doing there?"

"No doubt plotting with your enemies, the Huguenots and the Spaniards—for an entirely political object, I am sure."

"No, by God, no! Plotting, rather, against my honour, with Madame de Chevreuse! I tell you that the queen loves this infamous Buckingham."

The cardinal, although protesting that he could not believe this of the queen, incensed Louis XIII so skilfully with an account of a letter the queen was reported to have been writing all day that the king ordered the queen's apartments to be searched, determined to have her papers. He even went to the queen himself and told her that he had given a certain order to Séguier, the keeper of the seals, and after the king had left this official appeared himself. He searched all the furniture but found nothing. Finally he forced the sobbing queen to hand over the letter from her bosom, and took it to the king without reading it. Louis found that it was addressed to the King of Spain, Anne of Austria's brother, and was, not the love letter he had feared, but a complete plan of attack against the cardinal. The queen invited her brother and the Emperor of Austria to make a pretence—offended as they were by the policy of Richelieu, whose constant aim was to humble the house of Austria—of declaring war against France, and to lay down the dismissal of the cardinal as a condition of peace; but of love, there was not one single word in all the letter.

The king, in great delight, inquired whether the cardinal was still at the Louvre. The answer was that his Eminence was in his office awaiting his Majesty's commands. The king immediately hastened to him. "Here, duke," said he, "you were right and I was wrong. The whole intrigue is political, and love was not the subject of this letter. But, on the other hand, there is a good deal about you."

The cardinal took the letter and read it with the greatest attention; and when he had reached the end, he read it a second time.

Richelieu then threatened to resign, but the king managed to dissuade him. Richelieu then urged the king to make some amends to the queen for falsely accusing her of unfaithfulness. The king, while refusing to apologize, was persuaded to hold a ball—for the queen loved dancing. Richelieu subtly suggested it would be an opportunity for her to wear the diamond studs given to her by the king.

On the eighth day after that the cardinal received a letter with the London stamp, and containing only these few lines:

> I have got them but cannot leave London for want of money.
> Send me five hundred pistoles, and, four or five days after having received them, I shall be in Paris.

On the very day that the cardinal received this letter, the king asked him what day he should hold the ball.

Richelieu counted on his fingers, and said to himself in a low voice:

"She will reach Paris, she says, four or five days after receipt of the money. Four or five days will be required for the money to get there; four or five days for her to return.

Allow for contrary winds and accidents of fate, and the weakness of a woman and let us fix it at twelve days."

"Well, duke," said the king, "have you calculated?"

"Yes, sire: this is the 20th of September; the city magistrates give an entertainment of the 3rd of October. That will suit wonderfully, for you will not appear to have gone out of your way to please the queen." Then the cardinal added, "By the way, sire, do not forget to tell her Majesty, the evening before the ball, that you wish to see how the diamond studs become her."

It was the second time that the cardinal had recalled the king's attention to these diamond studs. His Majesty had been struck by his insistence, and supposed that the recommendation concealed some mystery.

More than once had his Majesty been annoyed that the cardinal's police—which, without having attained the perfection of modern times, were nevertheless very good—were better informed than he himself of what was taking place in his own royal household. He went, therefore, at once to see the queen and asked her to be sure to wear the diamond studs he had given her for her birthday when she went to the ball. The queen went pale, realizing that Richelieu must know all, and after the king had departed she sank down on to a cushion and prayed, with her head buried between her palpitating arms. Her position was, in fact, terrible. Buckingham had returned to London, Madame de Chevreuse was at Tours. More closely watched than ever, the queen felt painfully certain that one of her ladies had betrayed her, without knowing which. La Porte could not quit the Louvre. She had not a soul in the world in whom she could trust.

In the prospect of the ruin which was hanging over her and the desolation which she experienced, the queen gave way to tears and sobs.

"Cannot I be of any service to your Majesty?" said a voice full of gentleness and pity.

The queen turned eagerly for there could be no deception in the tone of that voice. It was the voice of a friend.

In fact, at one of those doors which opened into the queen's apartments appeared the pretty Madame Bonacieux. She had been engaged in arranging dresses and linen in a closet when the king entered, and, being unable to get out, had heard the whole of the conversation.

She told the queen that she knew of someone who would be able to help her by going to London at once to fetch the studs. Anne of Austria wrote a message of two lines, sealed it with her private seal and gave it to Madame Bonacieux, with a ring to sell to provide money for the journey.

Madame Bonacieux had intended her husband to be the messenger, but when she returned home she found he had become enthusiastically cardinalist, gloating over Richelieu's bag of money. She did not therefore reveal any details to him but she

had told him enough to make him leave at once to inform the
Count de Rochefort that the queen was trying to communicate
with someone in England. Left alone, poor Madame Bonacieux
was in despair. At that moment a knock on the ceiling made her
raise her head, and a voice, which came through the floor, called
out to her:

"Dear Madame Bonacieux, open the little door in the alley,
and I will come down to you."

6

A Hurried Visit to London

"Ah, madame," said d'Artagnan, as he entered the door which the young woman opened for him, "allow me to tell you that you have but a sorry husband."

"What! Have you heard our conversation?" eagerly demanded Madame Bonacieux, looking anxiously at d'Artagnan.

"Every word of it."

"But, good God, how could you?"

"By a method of my own, whereby I also heard the more animated conversation which you had with the cardinal's men."

"And what did you understand from what we said?"

"A thousand things. First, that, happily, your husband is a fool and a blockhead; in the next place, that you are in trouble. I am heartily glad of this since it gives me an opportunity of engaging myself in your service; and God knows I am willing to throw myself in the fire for you. Then, that the queen wants some brave, intelligent, and devoted man to go to London for her. I have, at least, two of the three qualifications which you require, and here I am."

Madame Bonacieux did not answer, but her heart beat with joy, and a secret hope sparkled in her eyes. "And what pledge will you give me," she demanded, "if I consent to entrust you with this commission?"

"My love for you. Come, speak, command: what is there to be done?"

"My God! My God!" muttered the young woman. "Ought I to confide such a secret to you, sir? You are almost a boy!"

But when d'Artagnan, with ardour in his eyes and persuasiveness in his voice, demanded that she should put him to the proof, the young woman, who was after all in one of those positions in which great risks must be run for the sake of everything, confided to him the terrible secret.

This was their declaration of mutual love. D'Artagnan glowed with joy and pride. This secret which he possessed, this woman whom he loved—the confidence and the love made him a giant.

"I am off," said he, "I am off directly."

"How are you going? And what about your regiment, your captain?"

"Upon my life, you made me forget all about them, dear Constance! Yes, you are right; I must get leave of absence."

"Another obstacle!" murmured Madame Bonacieux sorrowfully.

But d'Artagnan promised that he could obtain his leave of absence without difficulty, so Madame Bonacieux handed him the bag of money the cardinal had given to her husband.

"Egad!" cried d'Artagnan, "It will be doubly amusing to save the queen with his Eminence's money."

"You are an amiable and charming young man!" said Madame Bonacieux. "Depend upon it, her Majesty will not prove ungrateful."

"Oh, I am abundantly rewarded already!" said d'Artagnan. "I love you, and you allow me to tell you so; and even this is more happiness that I had dared to hope for."

"Hush!" said Madame Bonacieux, starting.

"What is the matter?"

"Someone is talking in the street."

"It is the voice—"

"Of my husband. Yes, I recognize it."

D'Artagnan ran and bolted the door. "He shall not enter till I am gone," said he; "and when I have left, you will open the door."

"But I ought to be gone too, and the disappearance of this money—how am I to explain it if I am here?"

"You are right—we must both go."

"Go? But how? He will see us if we go out."

"Then we must go up to my room."

"Ah," said Madame Bonacieux, "you say that in a tone that frightens me!" She uttered these words with tears in her eyes. D'Artagnan perceived the fears and threw himself upon his knees in deep emotion.

"On the word of a gentleman," said he, "in my room you shall be as safe as in a temple."

"Let us go then, my friend," said she, "I trust in that word."

D'Artagnan carefully unfastened the bolt, and both, light as shadows, glided through the door into the court, and, noiselessly ascending the stairs, entered d'Artagnan's chamber.

They saw M. Bonacieux talking to a man in a cloak. At the sight of him d'Artagnan made a spring and partly drawing his sword rushed towards the door—it was the man of Meung! Only with difficulty did Madame Bonacieux succeed in restraining him from rushing after the unknown, by reminding him that he was now in the queen's service. Reluctantly he let the two men enter M. Bonacieux's apartment, and, opening the hole he had made in the flooring, they heard Bonacieux telling the man in the cloak that his wife had an important mission to execute in England for an illustrious person, but that he knew no names. The man in the cloak went out, after urging Bonacieux to feign acceptance of the mission after all. Then M. Bonacieux discovered his money had gone and set up a terrible hullabaloo. Nobody came to his help so he went out, still uttering cries, which they heard gradually dying away.

"And now that he has gone, it is your turn to depart," said Madame Bonacieux. "Be brave, but above all, be prudent and remember that you serve the queen."

"The queen, and you!" exclaimed d'Artagnan. "Be assured, beautiful Constance, that I shall return worthy of her gratitude; but shall a return worthy, also, of your love?"

The young woman only replied by the glowing blush that

mounted to her cheek. After a few moments, d'Artagnan went out in his turn, enveloped in a long cloak, which was cavalierly thrust backward by the thrust of his enormous sword.

Madame Bonacieux followed him with that long look of affection which a woman fixes on the man she loves; but, as soon as he had turned the corner of the street, she sank upon her knees, and joining her hands, exclaimed:

"Oh, my God! Preserve the queen, and preserve me!"

D'Artagnan went straight to M. de Tréville. He had reflected that the cardinal would, in a few minutes, be put upon his guard by that cursed stranger, who appeared to be his agent, and he very wisely thought that there was not a moment to lose.

M. de Tréville was in his drawing-room, surrounded by his usual circle of gentlemen. D'Artagnan, who was known as an intimate of the house, went directly to his office, and asked to speak to him on business of importance.

He had scarcely been here five minutes before M. de Tréville entered. At the first glance, and from the joy which sparkled in d'Artagnan's eyes, the worthy captain at once perceived that some fresh scheme was in his mind.

"You sent for me, my young friend?" said M. de Tréville.

"Yes, sir," said d'Artagnan, "and you will pardon me, I hope for having disturbed you, when you know the importance of my business."

"Speak then. I am all attention."

"It is nothing less," said d'Artagnan, speaking low, "than that the honour, and perhaps the life, of the queen is at stake."

"What are you saying?" said M. de Tréville, looking round to be certain that they were alone.

"I say, sir, that chance has made me master of a secret."

"Which you will guard with your life, I hope, young man."

But which I ought to impart to you, sir; for you alone can assist me in the mission which has just been entrusted on behalf of her Majesty."

"Keep your secret, young man, and tell me what you want."

"I wish you to obtain for me, from M. des Essarts, a leave of absence for fifteen days."

"When?"

"This very night!"

"Do you leave Paris?"

"I go on a mission."

"May you tell me where?"

"To London."

"Has anyone an interest in preventing the success of your design?"

"The cardinal, I believe, would give anything in the world to prevent that success."

"And do you go alone?"

"Yes."

"In that case, you will not get past Bondy. It is I who tell you so, on the word of de Tréville."

"And why so?"

"You will be assassinated."

"I shall be doing my duty."

"But your mission will not be performed."

"That is true," said d'Artagnan.

"Believe me," said M. de Tréville, "in every enterprise of this kind there ought to be four at least, in order that one may succeed."

D'Artagnan saw the sense in the suggestion and three very surprised musketeers received leave of absence for fifteen days, ostensibly to accompany Athos while he took the waters of Forges to help to cure his wound. D'Artagnan explained to them that in reality they had to go to London with an urgent and secret letter but did not tell them what was in it. They discussed various ways of getting there and of avoiding the dangers they were sure to find, and then Athos said:

"I am going to take the waters, and you will accompany me; but instead of going to Forges I am going to the sea: I may take my choice. If anybody wants to arrest us, I show M. de Tréville's letter, and you will show your leaves of absence; if they attack us, we will defend ourselves; if they interrogate us, we must maintain sharply that we had no other intention than to dip ourselves a certain number of times in the sea. They would have too easy a conquest over four separate men; whilst four men united make a troop. We will arm our four servants with carbines and pistols; and if they send an army against us, we will give battle. As d'Artagnan says, if he should be killed, another must take the letter and pursue the route; if he is killed, it is another's turn and so on. Provided a single one arrives, that is all that is necessary."

"Well done!" said Aramis. "You do not speak often, Athos, but when you do speak, it is like St. John of the golden mouth. I agree to Athos's plan."

"And you, Porthos?"

"And I also," said Porthos, "if it suits d'Artagnan. As the bearer of the letter he is naturally the leader of the enterprise. Let him decide, and we will execute."

"Well, then," said d'Artagnan, "I decide that we adopt Athos's plan, and that we set out in half an hour."

"Agreed!" exclaimed the three musketeers in chorus.

And each, plunging his hand into M. Bonacieux's money-bag, took from it a share of the pistoles, and made his preparations to depart at the appointed time.

At two o'clock in the morning our four adventurers left Paris. Whilst the night lasted they remained silent. In spite of themselves, they felt the influence of the darkness, and suspected an ambuscade at every step.

With the first streak of day, their tongues became unbound, and gaiety returned with the sun.

The appearance of the cavalcade was most formidable; the black horses of the musketeers, their martial bearing, and that military custom which made these noble chargers march in rank, were all indications of their calling, which would have betrayed the strictest incognito. The valets followed, armed to the teeth.

All went well as far as Chantilly, where they arrived at about eight in the morning, and where they were obliged to breakfast. They dismounted at a tavern which was recommended by the sign of St. Martin giving half his cloak to a beggar. They ordered their servants not to unsaddle the horses, and to be ready to depart at a moment's notice.

They entered the public room of the inn and seated themselves at table. A gentleman was seated at the table, breakfasting. He entered into conversation concerning the rain and the fine weather. The travellers replied; he drank to their healths, and they returned his politeness. But at the moment when Mousqueton came to announce that the horses were ready, and they were rising from the table, the stranger proposed to Porthos to drink the cardinal's health. Porthos replied that he desired nothing better, provided the stranger would, in turn, drink the health of the king. The stranger replied that he knew no other king than his Eminence. On this, Porthos told him he must be drunk, and the stranger drew his sword. The argument was to be settled only by a duel.

The others had to leave Porthos at Chantilly; there was no help for it. They told him to rejoin them after his duel, and then proceeded on their way.

At Beauvais they stopped two hours, as much to breathe their horses as to wait for Porthos. At the end of that time, as neither Porthos nor any news of him had arrived, they resumed their journey.

About a league from Beauvais, at a point where the road was narrowed between two banks, they met eight or ten men, who, taking advantage of the road being unpaved at this place, seemed to be engaged in digging holes and making muddy ruts. Aramis, not liking to soil his boots, complained sharply at them. The men replied by seizing muskets hidden in the ditch and firing at them. Aramis received a ball which passed through his shoulder and Mousqueton fell from his horse, slightly wounded, but the others all galloped away.

They galloped on for two more hours, although the horses were so fatigued that it was to be feared that they would break down on the way.

The travellers had made a detour by side roads, hoping to be less molested; but at Crèvecœur Aramis declared that he could go no farther. In fact, it had required all the courage which he concealed beneath his elegant form and polished manners to proceed so far. At each movement he grew paler; and they were at last obliged to support him on his horse. Putting him down at the door of an inn, and leaving him with Bazin, who was more hindrance than help in a skirmish, they set off again in hopes of reaching Amiens, and passing the night there.

"Zounds!" said Athos, when they found themselves once more upon the way, reduced to two masters with Grimaud and Planchet. "I will be their dupe no more. I promise you that they shall not make me open my mouth or draw my sword, between here and Calais. I swear—"

"Don't swear," said d'Artagnan, "but gallop; that is, if our horses will consent to it."

And the travellers dug their spurs into the flanks of their horses, which, thus urged, recovered some of their strength. They reached Amiens at midnight, and dismounted at the sign of the Golden Lily.

They declined the rooms the innkeeper offered as they were at opposite ends of the inn. They decided to sleep in the public room, with Planchet guarding them and Grimaud guarding the stable. But Grimaud was knocked senseless by the ostlers during the night and next morning Athos was trapped by four men while paying the bill in the innkeeper's room. D'Artagnan and Planchet, given the alarm by Athos's shouts, galloped away at once, leaving Athos to fight it out.

Spurring on as fast as possible, they reached St. Omer where they gave their horses a rest, with their bridles looped on their arms for fear of accidents, and ate a morsel standing in the street; after which they again set off.

At a hundred paces from the gate of Calais, d'Artagnan's horse fell, and could not be made to get up again. Planchet's horse still remained; but he had chosen to halt and nothing could induce him to continue his exertions. Fortunately, as we have said, they were only a hundred paces from the town. They therefore left the two horses upon the highway, and ran to the harbour. Planchet called his master's attention to a gentleman who had just arrived with his lackey and was about fifty yards in front of them.

They hastily drew near this gentleman, who appeared to be in a great hurry. His boots were covered with dust and he was inquiring whether he could cross to England instantly.

"Nothing easier," replied the master of a vessel then ready for sailing, "but an order arrived this morning to let no one leave without permission from the cardinal."

"I have that permission," said the gentleman, drawing a paper from his pocket. "There it is."

"Get it countersigned by the governor of the port," said the master of the vessel, "and give me the preference."

"Where shall I find the governor?"

"At his country house."

"And where is his country house?"

"At a quarter of a league from the town: see, you may see it from here—that slated roof, at the foot of that little hill."

"Very well," said the gentleman; and followed by his servant, he took the road to the governor's country house. D'Artagnan and Planchet followed him, at the distance of five hundred yards.

Once out of the town, d'Artagnan hurried forwards and, making up on him as he entered a small wood, civilly demanded of the gentleman to allow them to cross the Straits before him. The gentleman refused, so d'Artagnan forced a duel, in which he ran his adversary through in four places. He found from his papers that his opponent was the Count de Wardes. Then, leaving the count insensible, and his servant Lubin bound and gagged in the wood, he proceeded to the governor as if he were Count de Wardes. The governor told him the port was shut against a certain d'Artagnan. Our Gascon told the governor that he knew d'Artagnan well and gave an exact description of the Count de Wardes. Grateful for this information, the Governor counter-signed the permission and in five minutes d'Artagnan and Planchet were on board the vessel.

It was time, for when they were half a league out at sea, d'Artagnan saw a flash and heard a detonation; it was the sound of the cannon that announced the closing of the port.

D'Artagnan was overpowered with fatigue. A mattress was spread on the deck for him, he threw himself upon it and slept.

The next morning at break of day, they were still three or four leagues from the shores of England. The wind had been gentle during the night, and they had made but little progress. At ten o'clock they cast anchor in the harbour of Dover, and at half past ten d'Artagnan landed in England, exclaiming:

"Here I am at last."

But this was not enough; he must get to London. D'Artagnan and Planchet each took a post-horse; a postilion galloped before them; and in a few hours they reached the gates of London.

D'Artagnan knew nothing of London; he knew not one word of English; but he wrote the word *Buckingham* on a piece of paper, knowing that anyone could direct him to the duke's man-sion. In this way he learned that the duke was hunting, at Wind-sor, with the king.

D'Artagnan then inquired for the duke's confidential valet, who, having accompanied him in all his journeys spoke French perfectly. To him he explained that he came from Paris on an affair of life and death, and that he must speak with his master without an instant's delay.

The confidence with which d'Artagnan spoke satisfied Patrick (for that was the name of the minister's minister). He ordered two horses to be saddled, and took upon himself the charge of guiding the young guardsman. As for poor Planchet, they had taken him off his horse as stiff as a stake. The poor fellow was exhausted; but d'Artagnan seemed to be made of iron.

They reached Windsor Castle where they learned that the king and the duke were out hawking in some marshes two or three miles off. In twenty minutes they reached the place. Patrick heard his master's voice, calling his hawk.

"Whom shall I announce to my lord?" said Patrick.

"The young man," said d'Artagnan, "who sought a quarrel with him one evening on the Pont Neuf."

Buckingham at once remembered d'Artagnan; and fearing that something had happened in France, of which information had been sent to him, he rode at fall speed straight up to d'Artagnan. Patrick kept himself judiciously in the background.

"No misfortune has befallen the queen?" cried Buckingham.

"I think not, sir; but I believe that she is in great danger, from which your Grace alone can rescue her."

"I!" said Buckingham. "What is it? I should be only too happy to render her any service. Speak, speak!"

"Take this letter," said d'Artagnan.

"This letter! And from whom comes this letter?"

"From her Majesty, I believe."

"From her Majesty," said Buckingham, growing so pale that d'Artagnan thought he was about to fall; and he broke the seal. "What is this rent?" asked he, showing d'Artagnan a place where it was pierced through.

"Ah!" said d'Artagnan. "I did not perceive it before: the sword of the Count de Wardes must have done that, when he ran it into my breast."

"Are you wounded?" inquired Buckingham.

"Oh! A mere trifle," said d'Artagnan, "a mere scratch."

"Just Heaven! What have I read?" exclaimed Buckingham. "Patrick, find the king, wherever he may be, and tell his Majesty that I humbly beseech him to excuse me, but an affair of the greatest importance calls me to London. Come, sir, come."

And both took their way to the capital at full gallop while d'Artagnan told him all he could about the queen and impressed Buckingham greatly by his description of the journey.

On entering the courtyard of his mansion, Buckingham jumped off his horse and rushed through magnificently decorated rooms until he came at last to a bedchamber, which was at once a miracle of taste and splendour. In the alcove of this chamber there was a door in the tapestry, which the duke opened by a small golden key, which he carried suspended at his neck. Buckingham perceived the hesitation of the young man.

"Come in," said he, "and if you have the happiness to be admitted into the presence of the queen of France, tell her what you have seen."

They found themselves in a small chapel, splendidly illuminated by wax lights, and carpeted with Persian silk carpets, embroidered with gold. Above a kind of altar, and under a dais of blue velvet, surmounted by red and white plumes, there was a life-size portrait of Anne of Austria, so perfectly resembling her that d'Artagnan uttered a cry of surprise on seeing it. On the altar, and under the portrait, was the casket which contained the diamond studs.

The duke approached the altar, and kneeling as a priest might do before the cross, opened the casket.

"Here," said he, drawing from the casket a large bow of blue ribbon all glittering with diamonds, "are those precious studs, which I had taken an oath should be buried with me. The queen gave them to me, she now takes them away: her commands, like those of Heaven, shall be obeyed in everything."

Then he began to kiss, one by one, the diamonds from which he was about to part; but suddenly he uttered a terrible cry.

"What is the matter?" demanded d'Artagnan, in alarm; "what has befallen you, my lord?"

"All is lost!" said Buckingham, becoming as pale as death.

"Two of the studs are gone; there are but ten."

"Has your Grace lost them, or do you suppose that they have been stolen?"

"Someone has stolen them," replied the duke; "and it is the cardinal who has managed it. See, the ribbons which held them have been cut with scissors."

"Has your Grace any suspicion as to who has committed the theft? Perhaps the person has still got them."

"Stop, stop!" said the duke. "The only time I have worn these studs was at a ball at Windsor, a week ago. The Countess de Winter, with whom I had had a quarrel, approached me during the ball. This appearance of reconciliation was really the vengeance of an offended woman. Since that day I have not seen her. That woman is an agent of the cardinal's!"

"What! Has he agents all over the world?" asked d'Artagnan.

"Oh, yes!" replied Buckingham, grinding his teeth with rage. "He is a terrible adversary. But when is this ball to take place?"

"Next Monday."

"Next Monday! Five more days! It is more time than we shall need. Patrick!" exclaimed the duke, opening the door of the chapel.

Buckingham called for his jeweller and his secretary. To the latter he gave an order stopping all English ships leaving for France. He then ordered his jeweller to make two studs exactly like those on the blue ribbon, keeping him prisoner until they were finished, but paying him liberally in addition to the price of the studs, for the annoyance. D'Artagnan stayed with Buckingham until they were finished. He refused all offers of reward from him as Buckingham was English and he was carrying out this commission in loyalty not to him but to Anne of Austria. Handing him the casket containing the twelve studs, Buckingham told d'Artagnan to take the brig *Sund* to St. Valéry and on his arrival to go to a sailors' lodging-house and repeat the password "Forward'. Relays of horses would then take him back to Paris. Buckingham urged him at least to accept these horses for himself and his three friends.

On reaching the brig *Sund,* d'Artagnan felt certain that he had seen the lady of Meung, who had been called my lady by the unknown gentleman, on board another vessel waiting to sail.

The next morning, about nine o'clock, he landed at St. Valéry. He immediately went to the appointed inn, pushed through the crowd to the host, and pronounced the word "Forward". The host made a sign to follow him, went out to the stables, where there stood a horse, ready saddled, and then asked d'Artagnan whether he needed anything else.

"I want to know the road I am to take," said d'Artagnan.

"Go from here to Blangy, and from Blangy to Neufchâtel. At Neufchâtel go to the tavern of the Golden Harrow; give the password to the innkeeper, and you will find, as here, a horse ready saddled."

"Have I anything to pay?" asked d'Artagnan.

"Everything is paid," said the host, "and most liberally. Go, then, and God protect you!"

"Amen!" said the young man as he galloped off.

In four hours he was at Neufchâtel. The same thing occurred there and at Ecouis, near Rouen, and again at Pontoise, and at nine o'clock he entered M. de Tréville's courtyard, at full gallop. He had covered nearly sixty leagues in twelve hours.

M. de Tréville received him just as though he had seen him the same morning, only pressing his hand a little more warmly than usual.

7

A Disappointed Lover

The next morning nothing was talked of in Paris but the ball which the magistrates were to give the king and queen, and in which their Majesties were to dance the famous ballet of *The Merlaison,* which was the king's favourite ballet.

For the last week every preparation had been in progress at the City Hall for this important entertainment. The guests began to arrive at six o'clock. The lady of the first president arrived at nine o'clock. As she was, next to the queen, the most distinguished personage of the entertainment, she was received by the city officials, and conducted to a box opposite to that of the queen.

At ten o'clock a collation of sweetmeats was prepared for the king. At midnight, loud cries and multitudinous acclamations resounded through the streets. It was the king who was proceeding from the Louvre to the City Hall, along thoroughfares illuminated throughout their length by coloured lamps.

The magistrates, clothed in their robes of cloth, and preceded by six sergeants, each holding a torch in his hand, hastened to receive the king, whom they met upon the steps where the provost of the merchants complimented and welcomed him; to which his Majesty replied by excuses for the lateness of his arrival, for which he blamed the cardinal, who had detained him till eleven o'clock, discoursing on affairs of state.

His Majesty, in full dress, was accompanied by his Royal

Prior, the Duke de Longueville, the Duke d'Elbeuf, the Count d'Harcourt, the Count de la Roche-Guyon, M. de Liancourt, M. de F radas, the Count de Cremail and the Chevalier de Souveray.

Everyone remarked that the king looked preoccupied and unhappy.

Half an hour after the arrival of the king, fresh acclamations resounded: these announced the arrival of the queen. The magistrates went through the same formalities as before, and preceded by their sergeants, advanced to meet their illustrious guest.

The queen entered the room; and it was remarked that, like the king, she looked sad, and also weary.

The moment that she entered, the curtain of a small gallery, which had till then been closed, was opened, and the pale face of the cardinal appeared. He was dressed as a Spanish cavalier. His eyes fixed themselves on the queen's and a smile of terrible joy passed over his lips. The queen was there without her diamond studs. Suddenly the king appeared, with the cardinal, at one of the doors of the saloon. The cardinal spoke to him in a low voice and the king was very pale.

The king broke through the crowds, and without a mask, and with the ribands of his doublet scarcely tied, approached the queen and in an agitated voice, said:

"Madame, why have you not on your diamond studs, when you knew it would have given me so much pleasure?"

The queen looked around her, and saw, behind the king, the cardinal smiling with a diabolical smile.

"Sire," replied the queen in a faltering voice, "because, amidst this crowd, I feared some accident might befall them.

"There you were wrong, madame. I made you this present in order that you might adorn yourself with it. I tell you that you were wrong."

The voice of the king trembled with anger. Everyone looked and listened with astonishment, not at all understanding this extraordinary scene.

"Sire," said the queen, "I can send for them to the Louvre,

where they are; and thus the wishes of your Majesty will be complied with."

"Do so, madame, and that immediately; for in one hour the ballet will begin."

The queen bowed submissively, and followed the ladies who were to conduct her to her closet. The king also retired to his.

There was a momentary excitement and confusion in the saloon. Everyone had perceived that something had occurred between the king and queen; but both of them had spoken so low that, as all had kept at a respectful distance, no one had heard anything. The violins began to play most strenuously, but no one attended to them.

The king left his closet first. He wore a most elegant hunting dress, and his brother and the other nobles were dressed in the same costume. This was the kind of dress most becoming to the king, and thus habited, he truly seemed the first gentleman of his realm.

The cardinal approached the king and gave him a box, in which his Majesty found two diamond studs.

"What does this mean?" demanded the king.

"Nothing' answered the cardinal; "only, if the queen has the studs, which I must doubt, count them, sire, and if you only find ten, ask her Majesty who can have robbed her of the other two."

The king looked at the cardinal as if to ask what this meant; but he had no time to put any further questions. An exclamation of admiration burst from every lip. If the king appeared to be the first gentleman of his realm, the queen was most indisputably the most beautiful woman in France.

True, of course, her huntress's costume fitted her most charmingly. She wore a beaver hat with blue feathers, a robe of pearl-grey velvet fastened with diamond clasps, and a skirt of blue satin embroidered with silver. Over her left shoulder glittered the diamond studs, suspended by a bow of the same colour as the feathers and the skirt.

The king trembled with joy and the cardinal with anger. Yet, at the distance they were from the queen, they could not count the studs; and although the queen had them, the question was, were there ten or twelve?

At this moment the violins sounded the signal for the ballet. It lasted an hour, and after it the king advanced quickly towards the queen.

"I thank you, madame," said he, "for the deference you have paid to my wishes: but I believe you have lost two studs and I bring them to you."

At these words, he offered her the two studs he had received from the cardinal.

"What, sire," cried the queen, affecting surprise, "do you give me two more? Why, that will make me have fourteen!"

In fact, the king counted them, and found the twelve studs upon her Majesty's shoulder. He summoned the cardinal. "Well, what does all this mean, cardinal?" he demanded in a severe tone.

"It means, sire," answered the cardinal, "that I wished her Majesty to accept these two studs; but not daring to make her the offer myself, I adopted this method."

"And I am the more grateful to your Eminence," replied Anne of Austria with a smile which proved that she was not the dupe of this ingenious gallantry, "as I am certain that these two studs have cost you more than the other twelve cost his Majesty."

D'Artagnan had watched the ball and was going to retire, when someone lightly touched his shoulder. He turned and saw a young woman who made a sign that he should follow her. Despite her mask he immediately recognized his usual guide, the gay and witty Madame Bonacieux.

They had met the previous evening, but only for an instant. The anxiety of the young woman to communicate the good news of her messenger's fortunate return to the queen, prevented the two lovers from exchanging more than a few words. On this account, d'Artagnan followed Madame Bonacieux, influenced by the double sentiment of love and curiosity. She hastily led him to a darkened closet, where she left him by a second door, through which flooded a brilliant light.

D'Artagnan remained an instant motionless, and wondering where he was; but shortly a ray of light and the warm and perfumed air penetrating from the next chamber, and the conversation of two or three women in language at once respectful and elegant, in which the word Majesty was frequently repeated, clearly indicated to him that he was in a closet adjoining the queen's apartment. The young man kept himself in the shadow, and listened.

The queen appeared gay and happy, which seemed greatly to astonish the ladies who surrounded her, who were accustomed to see her always full of care.

Suddenly, a hand and arm of an adorable colour were passed through the tapestry. D'Artagnan comprehended that this was his reward: he threw himself upon his knees, seized this hand, respectfully pressed his lips upon it, and then it was withdrawn, leaving in his what he perceived to be a ring. The door was immediately shut, and d'Artagnan was again left in complete darkness.

He put the ring upon his finger and once more waited.

The neighbouring chamber emptied gradually, after which the door of the closet was opened, and Madame Bonacieux entered quickly.

"You at last!" cried d'Artagnan.

"Silence!" said the young woman putting her hand upon his hips; go out again the same way you came."

"But where and when shall I see you again?" cried d'Artagnan.

"A note which you will find at your lodgings will tell you. Go! Go!" And at these words she opened the door of the corridor, and pushed d'Artagnan out of the closet.

He obeyed like a child, without resistance or even objection, which proves very positively that he was in love.

D'Artagnan ran the whole of the way home; and although it was three in the morning, and he had to pass through the worst parts of Paris, he met with no misadventure.

On his return, Planchet told him there was a letter for him; the young man rushed into his chamber and opened it.

It was from Madame Bonacieux, and expressed in these terms:

> Warm thanks are to be given and transmitted to you. You
> must be at St. Cloud this evening at ten o'clock, opposite the
> pavilion that stands at the corner of M. d'Estrees' house.
>
> C.B.

On reading this letter, d'Artagnan felt his heart dilating and contracting in that delirious spasm which is the torture and delight of lovers. It was the first note he had received—the first appointment that had been granted to him. His heart, expanding in the intoxication of his joy, felt as though it would faint at the very gate of Love. He read his note over and over again, and kissed, at least twenty times, these lines traced by the hand of his beautiful mistress. At length he retired to bed, and slept, and was visited by golden dreams.

At seven o'clock in the morning, he rose, and called Planchet, who, at the second summons, opened the door.

"Planchet," said he, "I am going out, probably for the whole day; you are therefore free till seven o'clock in the evening; but you must be ready at that hour with two horses."

As he went out he exchanged a few words with M. Bonacieux.

He went towards M. de Tréville's; his visit of the evening before having been, as it may be remembered, very short, with few chances for explanations. He found M. de Tréville in the heartiest joy. The king and queen had been most gracious to him at the ball. The cardinal, it is true, had been very ungracious; at one o'clock in the morning he had retired, under the pretext of indisposition. As for their Majesties, they had not returned to the Louvre till six in the morning.

"Now," said M. de Tréville, lowering his voice, and looking cautiously around the room to be sure that they were alone, "my young friend, let us talk of yourself; for it is evident that your safe return is connected with the king's joy, the queen's triumph, and his Eminence's humiliation. You must look out for yourself."

"What have I to fear," answered d'Artagnan, "so long as I have the good fortune to enjoy their Majesties' favour?"

"Everything, believe me. The cardinal is not the man to forget being made a fool of, at least until he has settled accounts with the person who has made a fool of him; and that person seems to me to be a certain youth of my acquaintance."

"Do you believe that the cardinal knows that I am the individual who has been to London?"

"The devil! You have been to London! And is it from London you bring that beautiful diamond which glitters on your finger!"

"No. This diamond comes from the queen. She handed it to me herself in giving me her hand to kiss."

And d'Artagnan related to M. de Tréville how everything had occurred.

"Oh, women, women!" cried the old soldier. "I recognize them well by their romantic imaginations: everything which is at all mysterious, charms them. So you saw her arm, and that was all: you might meet the queen and not recognize her a She might meet you and not recognize you?"

"No; but thanks to this diamond—" replied the young man.

"Listen," said M. de Tréville. "Will you allow me to give you some advice—some good advice—a friend's advice?"

"You will do me honour, sir," replied d'Artagnan

Then M. de Tréville advised him to sell or conceal the queen's ring. He warned him that the cardinal would certainly wreak his vengeance on him and suggested he leave Paris as soon as his appointment was over, to the comparative safety of rural France. On hearing this, d'Artagnan decided to go in search of his three friends and took his leave of M. de Tréville, more than ever touched by his parental solicitude for his musketeers.

He went successively to the homes of Athos, Porthos and Aramis; but none of them had returned. Their servants were also absent, and nothing had been heard of either masters or lackeys.

In passing, he looked in at the stables. Planchet was busy

grooming the horses, and took the chance to warn his master that he distrusted M. Bonacieux, who had taken his hat and run off as soon as his conversation with d'Artagnan was over.

At nine o'clock, d'Artagnan found Planchet ready armed, with the horses. D'Artagnan had his sword, and placed two pistols in his belt. They each mounted, and set off quietly. It was a dark night and none saw them depart. Planchet followed his master at the distance of ten paces.

D'Artagnan passed over the quays, and proceeded along the charming road—far more beautiful then than now—which leads to St. Cloud.

As long as they were still in town, Planchet kept the respectful distance that he had fixed for himself; but when the road became darker and more lonely, he gradually drew nearer, so that, when they entered the Bois de Boulogne, he found himself quite naturally riding side by side with his master. In fact, we must not deny that the waving of the trees and the reflection of the moon amongst the sombre copses caused him much uneasiness.

D'Artagnan perceived that something more than usual was passing in the mind of his lackey, who was still perturbed about the traitorous look on M. Bonacieux's face. Planchet, indeed, showed so much fear that when they had left the Bois de Boulogne his master gave him a half pistole to feed himself, got on his horse, threw the bridle to Planchet, and hurried away, enveloped in his cloak.

"Good God! How cold I am!" exclaimed Planchet, as soon as he had lost sight of his master; and in such haste was he to warm himself that he hurried to rap at the door of an inn.

In the meantime, d'Artagnan, who had taken a side-road, reached St. Cloud; but instead of proceeding along the main street, he turned behind the castle, went down a narrow unfrequented lane, and soon found himself opposite the appointed pavilion. It was situated in a perfect desert of a place. A long wall, at the corner of which was the pavilion, ran along one side of this lane, and on the other a hedge hid from the wayfarer a small garden, at the bottom of which there stood a miserable cottage.

He had now reached the place of appointment; and as he had not been told to announce his presence by any signal, he waited.

Not a sound was heard; he might have fancied himself a hundred miles from the capital. D'Artagnan cast a glance behind him, and then leaned against the hedge. Beyond this hedge, garden and cottage, a heavy mist enveloped in its shade that vast immensity where Paris slept.

His eyes were fixed on the pavilion, of which all the windows were closed with shutters, except one upon the first floor. From this window there shone a soft light, which silvered over the trembling foliage of two or three linden trees. Doubtless, behind that little window, so kindly lighted up, pretty Madame Bonacieux awaited him. A lingering sentiment of diffidence restrained her; but now that the hour had struck the window would be opened, and d'Artagnan would at last receive from the hands of Love the meed of his devotion.

Flattered by this sweet belief, d'Artagnan waited a half hour, without any impatience, keeping his eyes fixed upon that charming little abode.

The belfry of St. Cloud proclaimed half-past-ten.

But, this time, without his knowing why, a shudder ran through his veins. Perhaps, also, the cold began to affect him, and he mistook for a mental impression what was in reality a sensation altogether physical.

Then the idea occurred to him that he had mistaken the hour of appointment, and that it must have been eleven instead of ten. He approached the window, placed himself under the ray of light, drew the letter from his pocket and read it again. He was not mistaken: the appointment was really for ten o'clock.

He resumed his post, becoming uneasy at the silence and solitude.

It struck eleven.

D'Artagnan began to fear that something really had happened to Madame Bonacieux.

He clapped his hands three times—the usual signal of lovers—but nothing, not even an echo, returned an answer. And then he thought, with some displeasure, that the young woman had perhaps fallen asleep whilst waiting for him.

He approached the wall and attempted to climb it; but the wall was newly rough-cast, and he broke his nails to no purpose.

At this moment he thought of the trees; and, as one drooped over the road, he fancied that if he climbed up it he might be able to see into the pavilion. In an instant he was among its branches, and through the clear glass of the window his eyes plunged into the interior of the pavilion.

But the quiet lamp cast its light upon a scene of frightful disarray. One of the window-panes was broken; the door had been forced open. Outside, there were the marks of feet and carriage wheels. Eventually, he noticed a woman's torn glove.

As d'Artagnan pursued these investigations, at every fresh discovery a more abundant and more icy moisture stood upon his brow; his heart was wrung with fearful anguish and his breath almost failed. Then he became almost frantic. He ran along the highway, hastened back along the road he had come by, and closely questioned the ferryman.

About seven o'clock in the evening, the ferryman said, he had ferried over a woman, enveloped in a dark cloak, who seemed to be exceedingly anxious to escape recognition; but, precisely on account of her precautions, he had been the more observant, and had discovered that she was young and pretty.

There were then, as now, crowds of young and pretty women, who came to St. Cloud, and had reasons for desiring to remain unseen; yet d'Artagnan doubted not for an instant that it was Madame Bonacieux whom the ferryman had brought across.

Everything concurred to prove to him that his presentiments were not groundless, and that some great misfortune had actually occurred. He ran back towards the castle, fancying that during his absence something else might have happened at the pavilion, and that some fresh instructions might be waiting for him there.

D'Artagnan then remembered that dark and wretched cottage, which had doubtless seen and might perhaps also speak. The gate was locked but he jumped over the hedge, and in spite of the barking of a chained dog, approached the cottage.

At his first summons no one answered. A death-like silence prevailed here as well as in the pavilion; yet as this cottage was his last resort, he persisted.

Eventually an old man came cautiously to the door. At first he refused to speak, then moved by the truth and grief in the young man's face as he told him his story, he described how three people had come at about nine o'clock, borrowed his ladder, sent a little, short, stout, elderly man, poorly dressed, up it to look in the window, and when he had whispered, "It is she!" they had broken in and taken a woman away by force. When he described the leader, d'Artagnan recognized the man of Meung.

D'Artagnan returned towards the ferry, almost heart- broken. Sometimes he could not believe that the victim was Madame Bonacieux, and hoped to find her the next day at the Louvre; sometimes he fancied that she had an intrigue with someone else who had surprised her and carried her off in a jealous fit. He doubted, sorrowed and despaired.

"Oh," cried he, "if only I had my friends here! At least then I should have some hopes of finding her; but who knows what is become of them?" It was almost midnight; the next thing was to find Planchet. He searched all the wine shops in the neighbourhood in vain; so he slept in one of the cafes until morning. He woke at six o'clock and the first thing he saw when he went out was Planchet with the horses as had been arranged.

Instead of returning home, d'Artagnan dismounted at M. de Tréville's door, and ran rapidly upstairs. This time he determined to tell him all that had occurred.

M de Tréville listened to the young man's recital with a gravity which proved that he saw something more in this adventure than a love affair; and when d'Artagnan had finished:

"Hum!" said he, "this savours of his Eminence a mile off."

"But what am I to do?" said d'Artagnan.

"Nothing, absolutely nothing just now; but leave Paris, as a have told you, as soon as possible. I will see the queen and tell her the details of this poor woman's disappearance, of which she is, doubtless, ignorant. These details will guide her; and, on your return, I may possibly have some good news to give to you. Trust to me."

Determined instantly to put M. de Tréville's advice into execution, d'Artagnan hastened towards the Rue des Fossoyeurs, to look to the packing of his portmanteau. On approaching No. 11 he perceived M. Bonacieux, in morning costume, standing at his door. Everything that the prudent Planchet had said the evening before about the sinister character of his landlord now recurred to d'Artagnan's mind, and he looked at him more attentively than he had ever done before. In fact, besides that yellow sickly pallor, which indicates the infiltration of bile into the blood and which might only be accidental, he remarked something craftily perfidious in the wrinkles of his face.

Bonacieux had splashes of the same mud on his shoes as d'Artagnan himself had on his boots. This made d'Artagnan wonder. He asked permission to fetch a glass of water from M. Bonacieux's apartment and thus was able to see that the bed had not been slept in. Bonacieux said he had been to the east of Paris, the exact opposite direction to St. Cloud. Now d'Artagnan was sure. The mercer must have been present at the abduction of his own wife.

In d'Artagnan's own room Planchet told him that M. de Cavois, Captain of the cardinal's guards, had come to bid him call on his Eminence. But this was so obviously a trap that they left Paris at once to search for Athos, Porthos and Aramis, Grimaud, Mousqueton and Bazin. D'Artagnan took with him a perfumed letter in an elegant handwriting that had come for Aramis.

Porthos they found at Chantilly, at the same hotel at which they had left him on the journey to London, recovering from his wounds. Aramis was at the tavern at Crèvecœur, discoursing on religion with two prelates, but his resolve to enter the Church vanished when d'Artagnan handed him his letter. D'Artagnan had to leave Aramis there as his wound was still hurting him severely. Bazin, who had been overjoyed at the prospect of his master becoming a bishop or perhaps a cardinal, was broken-hearted at his return to secular life. Having arrived at Amiens, d'Artagnan found Athos had barricaded himself with Grimaud in the cellars of the inn, where he had been ever since the morning d'Artagnan had left him. When he came out he was dead drunk—declaring he had drunk at least one hundred and fifty bottles of the wine stored in the cellars, to teach the innkeeper the lesson to treat his guests more courteously. Hearing that d'Artagnan thought himself the most unfortunate of men, he told him a real tale of love to explain why he did not think his disappointment over Madame Bonacieux was very important.

"One of my friends—not myself—" said Athos, interrupting himself with a sombre smile, "one of the counts of my province of Berry became enamoured at twenty-five years of age of a young girl of sixteen, who was as beautiful as love. Through the simplicity of her age, an ardent soul was perceptible; the soul, not of a woman, but of a poet. She did not merely please, she intoxicated. She lived in a small village with her brother who was a curate. They were newcomers into that part of the country. No one knew where they came from; and, on seeing her so beautiful, and her brother so pious, no one thought of inquiring. They were, however, said to belong to a good family. My friend, who was the great man of that neighbourhood, might have seduced her, or even seized her by force, if he had chosen. He was the master, and who would have thought of defending two unknown strangers? Unfortunately, he was a man of honour, and he married her. The fool! The ass! The idiot!"

"But why, since he loved her?" said d'Artagnan.

"Wait a little," replied Athos. "He took her to his castle and made her the first lady of the province, and, to do her justice, she filled her position admirably."

"Well?" said d'Artagnan.

"Well! One day when she was out hunting with her husband," continued Athos, speaking in a low voice and quickly, "she fell from her horse and fainted. The count hastened to her assistance, and, as she seemed half-suffocated by her clothes, cut them with his dagger, so that her shoulder was exposed. Guess what was there upon her shoulder, d'Artagnan?" said Athos, with a convulsive burst of laughter.

"How can I tell?" demanded d'Artagnan.

"A fleur-de-lis!" said Athos. "She was branded. The angel was a fiend—the simple young girl had been a thief."

"And what did the count do?"

"The count was a powerful noble; he had the undisputed right of executing justice on his own domain: he tore off the remainder of her dress, tied her hands behind her back and hung her on a tree!"

"Oh heavens, Athos, a murder!" cried d'Artagnan.

"Yes, a murder—nothing else!" said Athos, pale as death. His head then fell on his two hands; whilst d'Artagnan remained before him, overwhelmed with horror. "That has cured me of women—beautiful, poetic, fascinating women," said Athos, raising himself, and forgetting to preserve the mystery of an intervening count. "May God grant you as much! Let us drink."

"But her brother?" timidly asked d'Artagnan.

"Her brother?" replied Athos.

"Yes, the priest."

"Ah! I sought him to hang him also; but he was too quick for me, he had fled the evening before."

"And did anyone ever discover who the wretch was?"

"It was the first lover and accomplice of the girl: a fine fellow, who had pretended to be a curate, that he might get his mistress married and provided for. He must have been quartered, I trust, by this time."

"Oh, my God!" exclaimed d'Artagnan, stunned by this horrible adventure.

8

A Diabolical Mistress

Next day they set out for Paris, Aramis and Porthos joining them on the way.

On arriving in Paris, d'Artagnan could obtain no tidings of Madame Bonacieux. M. de Tréville had spoken of her to the queen; but the queen did not know what had become of her, and promised to have a search made. This promise, however, was vague, and did not reassure the troubled d'Artagnan.

Meantime, he found a note from M. de Tréville, informing him that his Majesty had just promised him his immediate admission into the musketeers.

Full of joy, he ran at once to his friends, whom he had only quitted half an hour before, and whom he found very melancholy, or rather, very anxious. They were in grand consultation at Athos's, which always indicated a concern of some importance.

They had, in fact, each received a note from M. de Tréville, telling them that as his Majesty intended to open the campaign on the first of May, they must immediately get their equipments ready.

The four philosophers looked at one another in great bewilderment; M. de Tréville never jested on a matter of discipline. How were they to raise the money to pay for their equipments?

Athos waited until d'Artagnan had gone out. "That diamond that glitters on our friend's finger! D'Artagnan is too good a comrade to leave his brothers in embarrassment while he wears a king's ransom on his middle finger? Let us wait and see what will happen."

Having said this, Athos did not quit his own apartment; he was determined not to take a single step to equip himself.

"There is a fortnight left," he said to his friends. "Well, if at the end of it I have found nothing, or rather, if nothing has come to find me, as I am too good a Catholic to blow out my brains with a pistol, I will seek a good quarrel with four of his Eminence's guards, or with eight Englishmen, and I will fight until one of them kills me; which, considering the number, cannot fail to happen. It will then be said that I died in the king's service; so that I shall have served him without having to furnish myself with an equipment."

Porthos continued to walk with his hands behind his back, saying, "I shall follow up my idea."

Aramis, thoughtfully and negligently dressed, said nothing.

It may be seen from these disastrous details, that desolation reigned throughout the little community.

The three friends—for as we have already said, Athos had sworn not to stir an inch in search of equipment—went out early, and came in late. They wandered through the streets, looking on every pavement to see if any passenger had dropped a purse. They might have been supposed to be following a trail, so watchful were they at every step. And when they met, their desponding looks seemed to ask of one another, "Have you found anything?"

Nevertheless, Porthos was the first to act. D'Artagnan saw him one day going towards the church of St. Leu, and instinctively followed him. Porthos entered the sacred edifice, after having twirled his moustache and pulled his imperial, which always portended, on his part, the most irresistible intentions. As d'Artagnan took some precautions to conceal himself, Porthos fancied that he had not been seen. D'Artagnan watched Porthos make eyes at a lady older than himself, rather yellow and slightly withered but still beautiful, and erect and haughty under her black hood. Porthos made eyes too at a fair lady near the choir, who was also a great lady, and whom, to his extreme surprise, d'Artagnan recognized as the lady of Meung—whom the unknown with the scar had addressed as "my lady'. In this way Porthos eventually fascinated the elder lady, Madame Coquenard, whom he already knew well, into promising to lend him enough money to purchase his equipment. He was to visit her and her husband of seventy-six, a solicitor, for dinner the next day, as a cousin from Noyon in Picardy.

D'Artagnan had followed the fair lady from the church without being observed by her. He saw her enter her carriage and heard the orders given to her coachman to drive to St. Germain. It was useless to attempt to follow, on foot, a carriage which was drawn by two vigorous trotting horses, and d'Artagnan, therefore, returned to the Rue Férou, after ordering Planchet to saddle two horses in M. de Tréville's stables.

Athos was at home, gloomily emptying a bottle of Spanish wine. He gave Grimaud a sign to bring a glass for d'Artagnan, and Grimaud obeyed with his habitual silence.

D'Artagnan related all that had occurred at the church between the solicitor's wife and Porthos, and how their companion was already in a fair way of obtaining his equipments.

"For my part," said Athos, in answer to this recital, "I am sure it will not be women who will bear the expense of my outfit."

"And yet, my dear Athos, handsome and refined, great noble as you are, neither princesses, nor queens even, are beyond what you might seek and win."

At this moment Planchet modestly thrust his head through the half-open door, and announced that the horses were there.

"What horses?" asked Athos.

"Two which M. de Tréville lends me, with which I am going to St. Germain," said d'Artagnan.

"And what are you going to do at St. Germain?" inquired Athos.

D'Artagnan then described how he had seen at the church that lady who, like the gentleman with the black cloak and with the scar upon his forehead, was ever in his mind.

"That is to say that you are in love with this lady now, as you were with Madame Bonacieux," ejaculated Athos, shrugging his shoulders as if in contempt of human weakness.

"Not at all!" exclaimed d'Artagnan. "I am only curious to penetrate the mystery with which she surrounds herself. I do not know why, but I fancy that this woman, unknown as she is to me and I to her, has an influence on my life."

Athos tried in vain to persuade d'Artagnan to give up Constance Bonacieux and amuse himself with my lady, so d'Artagnan bade him goodbye and he and Planchet got into their saddles, and took the road to St. Germain.

As they went along d'Artagnan could not help thinking of all that Athos had said of Madame Bonacieux. Although he was not of a very sentimental nature yet the mercer's pretty wife had made a very real impression on his heart. In the meantime he was going to try to find out who the fair lady was. She had talked to the man in the black cloak, and, therefore, she was certainly acquainted with him. Now, the man with the black cloak had, in d'Artagnan's opinion, certainly carried off Madame Bonacieux for the second time, as he had carried her off the first. D'Artagnan, therefore, was only telling half a lie, which is not much of a one, when he said that, in his pursuit of this lady, he was in a way to discover Constance. Meditating thus and touching his horse occasionally with the spur, d'Artagnan completed his journey to St. Germain. He had just skirted the pavilion, where, ten years afterwards, Louis XIV was to be born. He was passing through a solitary street, looking right and left to see if he could discover some trace of the beautiful Englishwoman, when on a ground floor of a pretty house, Planchet recognized a person walking on a sort of terrace ornamented with flowers.

"Eh, sir," said he, "do you not remember that face which is now gaping around over there?"

"No' said d'Artagnan; "and yet I am convinced it is not the first time that I have seen it."

"I believe you," said Planchet. "It is poor Lubin, the valet of the Count de Wardes, whom you settled so thoroughly a month ago at Calais, on the way to the governor's house."

"Oh, yes," said d'Artagnan, "I remember him now. Do you believe that he would recognize you?"

"Faith, sir, he was in such a fright that I doubt he could have a very clear recollection of me."

"Well, then," said d'Artagnan, "go and chat with him, and find out whether his master is dead or not."

Planchet dismounted and went up to Lubin, who did not recognize him; and the two valets began to converse together with the utmost good fellowship; whilst d'Artagnan backed the horses down a lane, and went round behind a house, so as to be present at the conference, concealed by a hedge of hazel bushes. After a minute's observation from behind the hedge, he heard the sound of wheels and saw the unknown lady's carriage stop in front of him. There could be no doubt about it, for the lady was inside. D'Artagnan bent down over his horse's neck that he might see everything, without being seen himself. The lady put her charming fair head out of the door, and gave some orders to her maid. This latter, a pretty girl, of from twenty to twenty-two years of age, alert and animated, jumped down from the step, on which she had been seated, and went towards the terrace where d'Artagnan had seen Lubin. D'Artagnan followed the maid with his eyes, but as it happened an order from the house had called Lubin away so that Planchet remained alone, looking to see where his master had concealed himself. The maid approached Planchet, whom she mistook for Lubin, and handed him a note.

"For your master," said she.

"For my master?" said Planchet in astonishment.

"Yes, and very urgent; take it quickly."

She then hastened towards the carriage which had already turned in the direction whence it had come, and jumped on the step; the carriage moved away. Planchet turned the note over and over again, and then, accustomed to passive obedience, he went along the lane, and met his master, who, having seen all, was hurrying towards him.

"For you, sir," said Planchet, handing the note to the young man.

"For me?" said d'Artagnan. "Are you quite sure?"

"I am quite sure of it; for the maid said "for your master" and I have no other master than you, so—A pretty slip of a girl that maid is, too, upon my word!"

D'Artagnan opened the letter and read:

A person who takes more interest in you than she will admit, would be glad to know what day you will be able to walk out in the forest. A valet, in black and red, will be waiting tomorrow, at the Hotel of the Field of the Cloth of Gold, for your reply.

"Oh, oh!" said d'Artagnan. "This is ardent. It seems that my lady and I are anxious about the health of the same person. Well, Planchet, how is this good M. de Wardes? He is not dead then?"

"No, sir; he is as well as a man can be with four sword wounds in his body, and he is still weak, having lost almost all his blood. Lubin did not know me and related to me the whole of our adventure."

"Well done, Planchet! You are the very king of valets Now mount your horse again, and let us overtake the carriage."

In about five minutes they saw the carriage standing in the road, and a richly dressed cavalier waiting at its door. The conversation between the lady and this cavalier was so animated that d'Artagnan drew up on the other side of the carriage without being observed by anyone but the pretty maid. The conversation was in English, which d'Artagnan did not understand; but the young man saw that the beautiful Englishwoman was enraged. He thought that now was the time to interpose; he therefore approached the other door and, taking his hat off respectfully, said:

"Madame, will you permit me to offer my services? It appears to me that this gentleman has offended you. Say one word, Madame, and I will immediately punish him for his want of courtesy."

At the first words the lady turned and looked at the young man with astonishment; and, when he had ended:

"Sir," said she, in very good French, "I would put myself under your protection with the greatest pleasure, if the person with whom I have quarrelled were not my brother."

"Ah, excuse me, then," said d'Artagnan, "I was not aware of that, Madame."

"What is that presumptuous fellow interfering about?" exclaimed the gentleman whom the lady had claimed as her brother, stooping to the top of the door. "Why does he not go about his business?"

"Presumptuous fellow yourself!" said d'Artagnan, bending down on his horse's neck, and answering through the other window. "I do not go because I choose to remain here."

The gentleman spoke a few words in English to his sister.

I speak in French to you, sir," said d'Artagnan; "do me the favour, then, to answer in the same language. You are the lady's brother, but happily you are not mine."

Surprisingly for this point in a quarrel, the lady coolly ordered the coachman to drive to the hotel. The pretty maid threw an anxious glance at d'Artagnan, whose good looks seemed to have made an impression on her. No material obstacle now intervened between the two men. The cavalier made as if to follow the carriage; but d'Artagnan seized his bridle and stopped him. "You perceive," said the Englishman, "that I have no sword with me. Would you show off your courage against an unarmed man?"

"I hope that you have one at home," said d'Artagnan; "if not, I have two, and will throw with you for one."

"Quite unnecessary," said the Englishman; "I am sufficiently provided with that kind of tool."

"Well, then, sir," replied d'Artagnan, "choose the longest and come and show it me this evening, behind the Luxembourg, at six o'clock. You probably have one or two friends with you?"

"Six o'clock. Yes, I have three friends who would consider it an honour to play the same game as myself. And now who are you?" demanded the Englishman.

"I am M. d'Artagnan, a Gascon gentleman, serving in the Guards, in the company of M. des Essarts: and you?"

"I am Lord de Winter, Baron of Sheffield."

"Well then, I am your humble servant, my lord," said d'Artagnan, "although your names are rather hard to remember."

D'Artagnan went straight to acquaint Athos, Porthos and Aramis with the affair in hand, and at the appointed time the friends proceeded with their four servants to an enclosure behind the Luxembourg, which was reserved for goats. Athos gave some money to the goatherd to keep out of the way; and the valets were ordered to do duty as sentinels.

A silent party soon came to the same field, and joined the musketeers; and then, according to the English custom, the introductions took place.

The Englishmen were all persons of the highest rank. The singular names of the three friends of d'Artagnan were, therefore, not only a subject of surprise to them, but also of disquietude.

"After all," said Lord de Winter, when the three friends had been named, "we do not know who you are, and we will not fight with men bearing such names. These names of yours are shepherds' names!"

"As you guess, my lord, they *are* false names," said Athos.

"Which makes us the more desirous of knowing your true ones," said the Englishman.

Athos then took aside the Englishman with whom he was to fight, and told him his name in a low voice. Porthos and Aramis did the same.

"You would have done well not to require me to make myself known," said Athos coolly to his adversary.

"Why so?"

"Because I am thought to be dead. I have reasons for desiring that it be not known that I am alive; therefore, I shall be obliged to kill you, that my secret may not be divulged."

The Englishman looked at Athos, thinking that he was joking. But Athos was not jesting at all.

"Gentlemen," said he, addressing his companions, and their adversaries, "are we all ready?"

"Yes!" replied as with one voice both English and French.

"On guard, then!" cried Athos.

And immediately eight swords were glittering in the rays of the setting sun, and the combat began with a fury that was natural enough between men who were doubly enemies.

Athos slew his opponent as he had foretold him, Porthos pierced his enemy's thigh and carried him to his carriage. Aramis pressed his adversary so hard that at last he ran away as fast as he could go.

As for d'Artagnan, he had simply and purely played a defensive game. Then, when he saw that his opponent was weary, by a vigorous thrust he disarmed him. The baron finding himself without a sword, retreated two or three steps; but his foot slipped as he stepped away, and he fell upon his back. With one bound d'Artagnan was upon him and, pointing his sword at his throat, said to the Englishman:

"I could kill you, sir, but I give you your life for your sister's sake."

D'Artagnan was overjoyed; he had accomplished the plan he had designed, the development of which illuminated his face with smiles.

The Englishman, enchanted with having to deal with so complete a gentleman, pressed d'Artagnan in his arms and complimented the three musketeers a thousand times. And then, as Porthos's adversary was already installed in the carriage, and Aramis's had run away, they had only to attend to Athos's victim.

"And now, my young friend—for I hope that you will permit me to call you by that name—" said Lord de Winter, I will, if agreeable to you, present you this evening to my sister, for I wish her ladyship to take you into her favour; and as she is not entirely without influence at court, perhaps a word from her may be useful to you hereafter." D'Artagnan glowed with delight, and gave an assenting bow.

As Lord de Winter left d'Artagnan, he gave him his sister's address. She lived at No. 6 in the Place Royale, which was at that time the fashionable part of the town. He also engaged to call for him in order to present him, and d'Artagnan made an appointment for eight o'clock, at Athos's apartments.

This presentation to "my lady' occupied all the thoughts of our young Gascon. He began by dressing himself out in a flaming style at home; and he then went to Athos, and according to his custom told him everything.

"What!" said Athos? "You have just lost a woman whom you thought good, charming, perfect, and here you are running after another!"

D'Artagnan felt the justice of the reproach. "I love Madame Bonacieux," said he, "with my heart; but I love my lady with my head; and by going to her house I hope to enlighten myself as to the character she plays at court."

But Athos warned him against her, for fear that she was a tool of the cardinal's, who would draw him into a trap. Then he went into another room.

Lord de Winter arrived at the appointed time. An elegant carriage was waiting at the door, and, as two excellent horses were harnessed to it, they were soon at the Place Royale.

Her ladyship received d'Artagnan graciously. Her house was furnished with remarkable splendour.

"You see," said Lord de Winter, as he presented d'Artagnan to his sister, "a young gentleman who had my life in his hands, but would not misuse his advantage, although we were doubly enemies, since it was I who insulted him, and since I am also an Englishman. Thank him, therefore, madame, if you have any good affection for me."

The lady slightly frowned; an almost imperceptible cloud passed over her brow; and then a smile so singular appeared upon her lips that the young man, who saw this triple change, almost shuddered.

Her brother observed none of it.

"Welcome, sir," said the lady, in a voice the singular softness of which contrasted strangely with the symptoms of ill-humour which d'Artagnan had just observed; "for you have this day acquired an eternal claim upon my gratitude."

The Englishman then turned towards them, and related all the circumstances of the combat. Her ladyship listened with the greatest attention; yet it was easy to see, in spite of her endeavours to conceal her emotion, that the account was not agreeable to her. The blood mounted to her face and her little foot trembled beneath her dress.

Lord de Winter perceived nothing of this. As soon as he had ended he filled two glasses with Spanish wine, and invited d'Artagnan to drink.

D'Artagnan knew that an Englishman regards it an insult to decline his toast. He went, therefore, to the table and took the second glass. But he had not lost sight of the lady, and by the aid of a mirror he was a witness to a change which took place in her countenance. Now that she thought she was unobserved, her features assumed an expression which almost amounted to one of ferocity.

The pretty maid then entered. She spoke a few words in English to Lord de Winter, who immediately begged d'Artagnan's permission to withdraw.

D'Artagnan shook hands with Lord de Winter, and turned to her ladyship. The countenance of this woman had, with a surprising power of change, resumed its gracious expression.

The conversation now became animated. Her ladyship explained that Lord de Winter was only her brother-in-law, and not her brother. She had married a younger son of the family, and was left a widow with a son. This child was the sole heir of Lord de Winter, if his lordship did not marry. All this exhibited to d'Artagnan a veil which concealed something, but he could not yet see beneath that veil.

After half an hour's conversation, d'Artagnan was quite convinced that her ladyship was his own countrywoman. She spoke French with a purity and elegance that left no room for doubt in that respect.

He uttered abundant gallantries and protestations of devotion; and, at all these fooleries that escaped from him, the lady smiled most sweetly. The hour for departure came at last, and d'Artagnan took leave of her ladyship, the happiest of men.

On the staircase he met the pretty maid, who, having brushed against him gently in passing, blushed to the eyes and begged his pardon in a voice so sweet that the forgiveness was at once granted.

D'Artagnan returned the next day, and received a still more favourable reception. Lord de Winter was not present, and it was her ladyship herself, on this occasion, who did the honours of the evening. She seemed to take a great interest in him, inquiring who he was and who his friends were; and whether he had not sometimes thought of attaching himself to the cardinal's service.

D'Artagnan uttered a fine eulogy of his Eminence, saying that he should not have failed to enter his guards, had he chanced to know M. de Cavois, instead of M. de Tréville.

The lady changed the conversation without the slightest affectation; and with the utmost apparent indifference of manner, asked him whether he had ever been in England.

He replied that he had once been sent over by M. de Tréville to negotiate for a supply of horses, and had even brought back four as a sample. In the course of this conversation her ladyship bit her lips three or four times: she had to deal with a youth who played a pretty close game.

D'Artagnan withdrew at the same hour as the previous visit. In the corridor he again met the pretty Kitty, for that was the maid's name.

He returned to her ladyship's on the next day, and the next again; and, on each occasion, my lady gave him a more flattering welcome. Every evening, too, either in the antechamber, in the corridor, or on the staircase, he was sure to meet the pretty maid. But d'Artagnan paid no attention to poor Kitty's strange persistence.

The duel, in which Porthos had played such a brilliant part, had not made him forget the dinner to which the solicitor's wife,

Madame Coquenard, had invited him. The next day, therefore, at about one o'clock, having received the last polish from Mousqueton's brush, he proceeded to the Coquenards' address. He was disappointed, the meal was extremely meagre. However, he haggled for a long time with Madame Coquenard about the money she would lend him to buy his equipment, and in the end it was agreed that the solicitor's wife should ask her husband for a loan of eight hundred livres in hard cash and should furnish the horse and mule which were to have the honour of bearing Porthos and Mousqueton upon their way to glory.

These conditions having been arranged, and the interest and time of payment stipulated, Porthos took leave of Madame Coquenard, and returned home, half-famished, and in a very ill-humour.

Now, d'Artagnan became each hour more deeply enamoured of her ladyship; nor did he ever fail to offer her a daily homage, to which the presumptuous Gascon was convinced that she must sooner or later respond.

As he arrived one evening, scenting the air like a man who expects a shower of gold, he met the maid at the carriage gate; but, on this occasion, the pretty Kitty was not contented with giving him a passing smile. She gently took his hand.

"I should be glad to say a few words to you, sir," she stammered, begging him to follow her. By the hand which she had continued to hold, Kitty then led d'Artagnan to a small, dark winding staircase; and after having made him ascend some fifteen steps, she opened a door. "Enter, sir, we shall be alone, and may converse here."

"And whose room is this then, my pretty child?" inquired d'Artagnan.

"It is mine, sir. It communicates with that of my mistress, through this door. But you may rely upon it she will not hear whatever we say, for she never goes to bed till midnight."

Kitty guessed what was passing in the young man's mind, and gave a sigh. "You are very fond of my mistress then. That is a great pity as my mistress does not love you at all."

"What!" exclaimed d'Artagnan. "Did she desire you to tell me so?"

"Oh no, sir, no! But I, from the interest I take in you, have resolved to tell you." Kitty drew from her bosom a small, unaddressed note.

"For me?" exclaimed d'Artagnan, as he hastily seized the letter, and, by a movement, quick as thought, tore off the envelope, in spite of the cry which Kitty uttered.

He read as follows:

> You have sent no answer to my first note. Are you, then, suffering too much, or have you forgotten the glances that you gave me at Madame de Guise's ball? Now is the opportunity, Count; do not let it escape you.

D'Artagnan grew pale: he was wounded in his vanity, but he believed it was in his love. "This note is not for me?" he exclaimed.

"No, it is for somebody else, the Count de Wardes."

The remembrance of the scene at St. Germain presented itself at once to the mind of the presumptuous Gascon, and confirmed what Kitty had that moment told him.

"Poor, dear M. d'Artagnan," said she, in a voice full of compassion, as she again pressed the young man's hand.

"You pity me, kind child," said d'Artagnan.

"Oh yes, with all my heart; for I know well what love is myself.

Kitty went on to explain that her mistress would never love him for he had grievously offended her by nearly destroying her credit with the cardinal. D'Artagnan guessed that it was over the matter of the studs. Suddenly her ladyship's bell rang. Kitty in a fright told him to leave, but d'Artagnan hid in a cupboard. He overheard my lady raging at Kitty, and later telling her how she hated d'Artagnan and would be revenged on him, though for some reason the cardinal had requested her to treat him kindly. A second reason for this hatred turned out to be that he had not killed Lord de Winter when his life was in his power. Then she herself would have had an income of three hundred thousand livres. In answer to Kitty's comment that her ladyship's treatment of Madame Bonacieux had not been very kind, my lady disclosed that she had taken vengeance upon her also. D'Artagnan realized now that this woman was a veritable monster.

Next day the infatuated Kitty brought d'Artagnan a second note which her mistress had written to de Wardes. He read it. Like the other, it bore neither signature nor address, and ran as follows:

> This is the third time that I have written to tell you that I love you: take care that I do not write a fourth time, to tell you that I hate you.

D'Artagnan's colour changed several times as he read this note, then he took up a pen and wrote:

> Madame, until now, I have been in doubt whether your former notes could really have been meant for me, so unworthy did I fed myself of such an honour; but today I must at last believe in the excess of your kindness, since not only your letter, but your servant also affirms that I have the happiness to be the object of your love.
>
> At eleven tonight I shall come to implore your forgiveness. To delay another day, at present, would be, in my opinion, to offer you a new affront.
>
> He whom you have rendered the happiest of mankind.

This note was not precisely a forgery, as d'Artagnan did not sign it, but it was an indelicacy: it was, even according to the standard of our present manners, something like an act of infamy; but the people of those times were less scrupulous that we are now. Besides, d'Artagnan knew from her ladyship's own avowal that she had been guilty of treacheries in important affairs, and his esteem for her was low.

As an interlude to his plans for revenge on her ladyship for her conduct towards both Madame Bonacieux and himself, d'Artagnan met his three friends. They had agreed to meet only once a week while searching for their equipments, and the day that Kitty gave him the note for the Count de Wardes happened to be one of these days. Aramis was in luck, as while they were together, a beggar—really a grandee of Spain in disguise—arrived with a note from Tours and one hundred and fifty Spanish double pistoles. Porthos was less fortunate. Mousqueton appeared bringing him the very yellow pony d'Artagnan had ridden from Tarbes to Paris. Angrily Porthos visited Madame Coquenard to complain about the frightful brute she had bought for him. She had a lame story to tell, of a horse-dealer who owed her husband money, had promised a noble steed, and then sent this yellow animal. She admitted she had done wrong, promised to make amends and they agreed to meet that evening.

The evening, so impatiently awaited by Porthos and d'Artagnan, at length arrived. At about nine o'clock, d'Artagnan went as usual to her ladyship's, and as he found her in a charming humour he was received more graciously than ever. Our Gascon saw, at the first glance, that the pretended note of the Count de Wardes had been delivered by Kitty to her mistress, and that it was producing its effect.

At ten o'clock her ladyship began to appear uneasy, and d'Artagnan guessed what this meant. She looked at the clock, got up, sat down again, and smiled at d'Artagnan, with a look which seemed to say, "You are very amiable no doubt, but you would be charming if you would go."

D'Artagnan arose and took his hat, and her ladyship gave him her hand to kiss. The young man was sensible of a gentle pressure, which he attributed, not to coquetry, but to gratitude on account of his departure.

"She loves him madly!" he murmured, as he went out.

On this occasion Kitty was not awaiting him, either in the antechamber, in the corridor, or at the gate; and d'Artagnan had to discover, alone, the staircase to her little room. Kitty was sitting there, her head hidden in her hands, and was weeping, dreading the consequences of her action. D'Artagnan waited in the wardrobe until the time for the arrival of the pretended Count de Wardes.

As the hour of her interview with the count approached, her ladyship had all the lights in her own room extinguished, and dismissed Kitty with instructions to introduce de Wardes as soon as he arrived.

Kitty had not long to wait. Hardly had d'Artagnan seen through the keyhole of his wardrobe that the whole apartment was in darkness, when he sprang from his hiding-place, at the very moment Kitty closed the communicating door.

"What is that noise?" inquired my lady.

"It is I," whispered d'Artagnan, "I, the Count de Wardes."

"Oh my God!" groaned Kitty. "He could not even wait for the hour he fixed himself!"

"Well," said my lady in a trembling voice, "why do you not come in? Come, count," she added, "you know that I am waiting for you."

At this appeal, d'Artagnan put Kitty gently aside, and sprang into her ladyship's chamber.

If rage and grief can ever torture the soul, it must be those of the lover who receives, under a name that is not his own, protestations of affection which are addressed to his favoured rival.

"Yes, count," said her ladyship in her sweetest tones, as she tenderly pressed one of his hands between her own; "yes, I am happy in the love which your glances and words have expressed whenever we have met. And I, too, return your love. Ah! Tomorrow you must let me have some souvenir, which will prove you think of me; and, as you might forget me, count, keep this."

And she slipped a ring from her own finger on that of d'Artagnan.

D'Artagnan remembered seeing that ring on her hand. It was a magnificent sapphire encircled by diamonds.

His first emotions prompted him to return it; but her ladyship added:

"No, no, keep this ring for love of me. Besides," added she in a voice of much emotion, "you really do me a far greater service by accepting it than you possibly can imagine."

"This woman is full of mystery," thought d'Artagnan.

He felt himself at this moment ready to confess everything. He had, in fact, already opened his mouth to tell her ladyship who he was, and with what vengeful desire he had come, when she added:

"Poor angel, whom that monster of a Gascon just missed killing."

That monster was himself!

"Do you still suffer from your wounds?" she continued.

"Yes, greatly," answered d'Artagnan, who was somewhat at a loss what to say.

"Depend upon it," muttered her ladyship, in a tone which gave but little comfort to her hearer, "that I will take a cruel vengeance on him for your sufferings."

"Egad!" said d'Artagnan to himself. "The time for my confession is scarcely come yet."

It required some little time for d'Artagnan to recover himself from this little dialogue. But all the ideas which he had brought with him had completely vanished. This woman exercised an unaccountable power over him: he hated and adored her at one and the same time.

But the clock had struck one and it was time for them to separate. At the moment of quitting her ladyship, d'Artagnan was only sensible of a deep regret at having parted from her; and in the passionate adieu which they mutually addressed to one another, a new meeting was agreed upon for the ensuing week.

The next morning d'Artagnan hastened to Athos; for, being engaged in such a singular adventure, he wished for his advice. He told him everything, and Athos's brow was often knitted during the narration.

"Your lady," said he, "appears to me to be an infamous creature; but you are not on that account the less wrong in thus deceiving her. You may now be sure that, in one way or another, you will have a bitter enemy on your hands." Whilst speaking, Athos gazed earnestly at the sapphire, encircled with diamonds, which d'Artagnan now wore in place of the queen's ring, which was carefully deposited in a jewel-case. A shadow of anger passed over his brow as he recognized the ring as one that had once belonged to him—an old family jewel, as he told d'Artagnan, which was never to leave his family.

"And you—sold it?" asked d'Artagnan with some hesitation.

"No," replied Athos, with a singular smile; "I gave it away during a night of love, even as it was given to you."

D'Artagnan grew pensive in his turn. He thought that he could discern in her ladyship's life abuses which were black and terrible in their depths. He put the ring, not on his finger, but in his pocket.

"Listen," said Athos, taking the young man's hand. "You know how much I love you, d'Artagnan. Had I a son I could not love him more dearly. Well, take my advice—renounce this woman. I do not know her, but a kind of intuition tells me that she is wicked, and there that is something fatal about her."

"You are right," said d'Artagnan, "and I will renounce her. I will confess that this woman frightens even me."

"And will you have the resolution?" asked Athos.

"Yes; and at once too," replied d'Artagnan.

"You are quite right, my dear d'Artagnan," said Athos, pressing his hand with an affection almost paternal; "and God grant that this woman, who has scarcely entered your life, may leave no pestilential trace upon it!" And Athos bowed his head, like a man who would rather be left to his own thoughts.

On reaching home, d'Artagnan found Kitty awaiting him. She had been sent by her mistress to the Count de Wardes.

Her mistress was mad with love—intoxicated with joy: she wanted to know when the count would accord her a second interview. The pale and trembling Kitty waited for d'Artagnan's reply.

Athos had considerable influence over the young man and d'Artagnan, fully resolved to see her ladyship no more, took a pen and wrote the following letter:

> Do not depend any more on me, madame. Now that I am becoming convalescent I have so many affairs of the same

kind to grant, that I must take them in a regular order. When
your turn comes round I shall have the honour to inform you. I
kiss your hands.

Not a word was said about the sapphire; the Gascon wished to
keep it for the present, as a weapon against her ladyship. But
Kitty was delighted with the letter.

Her ladyship opened the letter with an eagerness equal to that
with which the maid had brought it; but at the first words that she
read she became livid: then she crushed the letter in her hand,
and turned, with lightning in her eyes, to Kitty. "What is this letter?" said she.

"It is the answer to your ladyship's,' said the trembling Kitty.

"Impossible!" exclaimed the lady; "impossible that a gentleman should have written such a letter to a lady!" Then suddenly
she cried: "My God! Could he know—"

She checked herself, shuddering. She ground her teeth, became
ashen-pale and fainted. When she recovered, she motioned Kitty
who was attempting to open her dress, to leave the room.

In the evening, her ladyship gave orders that M. d'Artagnan
was to be admitted as usual, as soon as he should come. But he
did not come nor did he come the next day, either.

Kitty went to tell him all that had happened. This jealous anger
of her ladyship was d'Artagnan's revenge. On the third day Kitty
bore him a letter.

He opened it and read as follows:

> Dear M. d'Artagnan,
>
> It is wrong to neglect your friends, especially when about to
> part for so long a time. I and my brother looked for you in
> vain, both yesterday and the day before. Will it be the same
> this evening?
>
> Your very grateful,
>   Lady de Winter.

"This is all very plain," said d'Artagnan, "and I expected this
letter. My credit rises as that of the Count de Wardes falls." And
he sent word that he would call at nine o'clock.

At nine o'clock, d'Artagnan was at the Place Royale and was at once admitted.

He observed the lady with great curiosity. She was pale, and her eyes were heavy, either from weeping or from want of sleep. The customary lights in the room had been designedly diminished in number; and yet the young woman could not conceal the traces of the fever which had been consuming her for two days. D'Artagnan approached her with his usual gallantry; and she made a mighty effort to receive him, but never did a more agitated face contradict a more enchanting smile.

She was more affectionate than ever and confided in d'Artagnan that she had an enemy who had so cruelly insulted her that there was war to the death between them. D'Artagnan's love for her, which he had believed was extinct, awoke again in his heart. Bemused by her beauty, he said at once that his arm and his life were at her service. Her ladyship, laughing to herself at the way she played one enemy off against another, restrained his impetuous haste. She asked him to leave when her brother arrived, and to return at eleven o'clock. He spent the time walking round the Place Royale, and his thoughts became sober and normal once more. On his return to her ladyship, believing she now loved him for himself, he confessed the truth—that the Count de Wardes of last week and the d'Artagnan of tonight were one and the same person.

The imprudent young man expected a little storm, which would dissolve in tears; but he strangely deceived himself and his error was quickly apparent.

Pale and terrible, her ladyship raised herself up, and pushed d'Artagnan away, by a violent blow on the chest.

He held her back by her robe, in order to implore her pardon. But, with a powerful and resolute effort, she endeavoured to escape. In this effort, her robe gave way leaving her neck bare, and then on one of her beautiful uncovered shoulders, d'Artagnan, with inexpressible horror, perceived the fleur-de-lis—that indelible mark impressed by the degrading hand of the executioner.

"Great God!" he exclaimed, letting the robe fall; and he remained mute, and rooted to his place.

But my lady felt herself denounced by d'Artagnan's very horror. Doubtless he had seen everything. The young man now knew her secret, that terrible secret—of which the whole world was ignorant, except him!

She turned, no longer like a mere furious woman, but like a wounded panther.

"Ah, wretch," said she, "you have betrayed me like a coward! And you have learned my secret! You must die!"

And she ran to an inlaid casket on her toilet table, opened it with a feverish, trembling hand, drew from it a small dagger, with a golden hilt and a sharp and slender blade, and flung herself with one bound on d'Artagnan, her robe in shreds. D'Artagnan drew his sword, and as this was like a duel he gradually recovered his coolness.

"Well done, beautiful lady, well done!" said he, "but be calm, or I will draw a second fleur-de-lis on the other shoulder!"

"Wretch! Wretch!" howled her ladyship.

But, d'Artagnan, still seeking the door, kept himself on the defensive. He dashed out and bolted the door. Shouting to Kitty not to open it, he fled down the stairs and out of the house just as my lady screamed from the window to the porter: "Do not open!"

The young man escaped while she still menaced him with an impotent gesture. At the same moment that she lost sight of him she fell back senseless into her bedroom.

9

A Meeting with the Cardinal

D'Artagnan was so completely bewildered, that, without considering what would become of Kitty, he ran through half Paris and did not stop till he found himself at Athos's house. He knocked as if he would break down the door.

Grimaud opened it. "Hollo!" he cried. "What do you want?"

"Be silent, you villain!" said the young man; "I am d'Artagnan. Don't you know me? Where is your master?"

"You, M. d'Artagnan!" exclaimed Grimaud.

"Grimaud," said Athos, as he quietly emerged from his chamber in his dressing-gown, "I believe you are permitting yourself to speak!"

Grimaud then contented himself with pointing to d'Artagnan with his finger.

Athos, phlegmatic as he was, burst out into a fit of laughter, which was occasioned by d'Artagnan's wild appearance.

"Do not laugh, my friend," exclaimed d'Artagnan, as he followed Athos into his room; "In the name of Heaven, do not laugh! For upon my soul, I assure you that there is nothing to laugh at. Prepare to hear something perfectly incredible—unparalleled."

"Speak, then, speak," said Athos.

"Well, then," continued d'Artagnan, bending towards Athos's ear, and whispering, "her ladyship is branded with a fleur-de-lis upon her shoulder!"

"Ah!" exclaimed the musketeer, as if he had received a bullet in his heart.

"But are you quite sure," continued d'Artagnan, "that the other is really dead?"

"The other!" murmured Athos in a voice so faint as to be scarcely audible.

"Yes; she of whom you told me one day at Amiens?"

Athos groaned and his head fell upon his hands.

"This one," said d'Artagnan, "is a woman of from twenty-six to twenty-eight years of age."

"Fair, with clear blue eyes," said Athos, "of an uncommon brightness and with black eyelashes and eyebrows; tall and well-made. She has also lost a tooth, next to the eye-tooth on the left side. The fleur-de-lis is small, of a red colour, and as if somewhat effaced by layers of paste applied to it."

"Yes."

"And yet you say that this woman is English?"

"She is called "my lady" but she may yet be a Frenchwoman; Lord de Winter is only her brother-in-law."

"I must see her, d'Artagnan."

"Beware, Athos, beware. You tried to kill her: she is a woman who would willingly pay you back, and not fail."

D'Artagnan then told Athos the whole story and that he was sure my lady was an agent of the cardinal. He gave Athos the sapphire ring she had presented him with, as it had been his originally. Though at first Athos refused to take it or sell it, they agreed in the end to pawn it and share the money. Planchet had come to the house in search of his master and, as Athos now renounced his plan of seclusion, the two friends went off with their servants, heavily armed.

They pawned the ring and Athos was thus unexpectedly able to buy his equipment with his share of the money. Meanwhile Kitty had appeared at d'Artagnan's lodging trembling with terror and begging for protection from her mistress. They appealed to Aramis, who wrote a recommendation to Madame de Bois-Tracy, who was looking for a maid for one of her friends who lived in the provinces. Kitty told them that M. Bonacieux, who had been hanging about the entrance, had gone away in a hurry. She had seen him twice at her mistress's house. The four friends realized their danger—Bonacieux had obviously gone to report to the cardinal—and they left the house as soon as possible.

At the appointed hour they reassembled at Athos's house. Their anxiety about equipments had entirely disappeared but they had some fear about the future.

Suddenly Planchet entered bearing two letters, addressed to d'Artagnan. One was a little note, neatly folded lengthwise, with a pretty seal of green wax, on which was impressed a dove bearing a green bough. The other was a large square envelope, glittering with the terrible arms of his Eminence the cardinal-duke.

At sight of the little letter, d'Artagnan's heart bounded, for he thought he recognized the writing; and, though he had only seen that writing once, the memory of it was engraven in his heart's core. So he took the note and unsealed it hastily. It said:

> Walk out about six or seven o'clock, on Wednesday evening next, on the Chaillot road, and look carefully into the carriages as they pass. But if you value your own life, or that of those who love you, do not speak, do not make one motion which may show that you have recognized her who exposes herself to every ill, only to see you for an instant.

There was no signature.

"It is a snare," said Athos. "Don't go, d'Artagnan."

"And yet," said d'Artagnan, "I think that I know the writing."

"But it may be forged," said Athos. "At six or seven o'clock at this season, you would be as solitary on the Chaillot road as if you went to walk in the Forest of Bondy."

"But suppose we all go?" said d'Artagnan. "Surely they could not beat us all four, besides the four servants, the horses and our arms."

They decided all to go; the others would remain a short distance behind d'Artagnan.

"But this second letter," said Athos, "you forget that. And yet, I fancy, the seal indicates that it is worth opening."

D'Artagnan opened the letter and read:

> M. d'Artagnan, of the King's Guards, of M. des Essarts'
> company, is expected at the cardinal's palace, at eight o'clock
> this evening.
>
> La Houdinière,
> Captain of the Guards.

"The devil!" said Athos. "Here is an appointment far more disquieting than the first."

"I will go to the second after attending the first," said d'Artagnan. "One is at seven, and the other at eight. There will be time enough for both. Gentlemen, I have already received a similar invitation from his Eminence, through M. de Cavois. I neglected it; and the next day a great misfortune happened to me. Constance disappeared. Whatever may be the result, I will go."

"If you are determined," said Athos, "do it."

"But the Bastille?" said Aramis.

"Bah! You will get me out again," rejoined d'Artagnan.

"Certainly," replied Aramis and Porthos, with the greatest of coolness, and as if it had been the simplest thing in the world, "we will get you out again. But as we must be off the day after tomorrow, you would do better not to run the risk of getting in."

"Let us do better," said Athos; "let us not leave him throughout the evening. Let each of us, accompanied by three musketeers, wait at a gate at the palace. If we see any closed carriage that looks suspicious, coming out, we will fall upon it. It is a long time since we have had a skirmish with the cardinal's guards; M. de Tréville must think we are dead."

"Decidedly, Athos," said Aramis; "you were cut out to be the general of an army. What do you say to the plan, gentlemen?"

"Admirable," replied the young men in chorus.

They got ready and all presented a fine spectacle in their new equipments and mounted on their new horses. Porthos, on a very handsome jinnet, was resplendent with joy and pride.

Near the Louvre the four friends met M. de Tréville, returning from St. Germain. He stopped them to compliment them on their equipments, which drew around them in an instant a few hundred loafers. D'Artagnan took advantage of this opportunity to speak to him about the great letter, with the great red seal and ducal arms. It will be imagined that, of the other letter, he did not breathe a syllable.

M. de Tréville approved of the resolution he had formed and assured him that if he should not be seen again on the next day, he would find him, wherever he might be.

At that moment, a clock struck six. The four friends excused themselves, on account of an engagement, and set off.

A short gallop took them to the Chaillot road. The day was beginning to decline. Carriages were passing backwards and forward. D'Artagnan, supported by his friends at a little distance, looked eagerly into every carriage, but saw no face he knew.

After they had waited about a quarter of an hour and as the twilight thickened, a carriage, advancing at full speed, was seen upon the Sevres road. A presentiment announced to d'Artagnan that this carriage contained the individual who had made the appointment with him. The young man was himself astonished at the violent beating of his heart. Almost at the same instant a woman's head was visible at the window, with two fingers on the lips as if to enjoin silence, or to send a kiss. D'Artagnan uttered a faint cry of joy. This woman, or rather this apparition, for the carriage passed away with the rapidity of a vision, was Madame Bonacieux.

By an involuntary movement, and in spite of the caution he had received, D'Artagnan set his horse to a gallop, and in a few bounds was close beside the carriage; but the window was hermetically sealed—and the vision was no longer there.

D'Artagnan then remembered the warning: *If you value your own life, and that of those who love you, remain motionless as if you had seen nothing.*

He stopped therefore, trembling not for himself, but for the poor woman, who had evidently exposed herself to great danger by the appointment she had made.

The carriage proceeded on its way, and, still going at full speed, soon entered Paris and disappeared.

His three companions gathered round him. They had all distinctly seen a woman's head at the window, but none of them, except Athos, knew Madame Bonacieux by sight. Athos believed that it was really she whom they had seen; but having been less engrossed than d'Artagnan by that pretty face, he thought that he had seen a second head—and a man's—at the back of the carriage.

"If that is the case," said d'Artagnan, "they are undoubtedly conveying her from one prison to another."

It now struck half-past seven; the carriage had been twenty minutes behind the appointed time. His friends reminded d'Artagnan that there was another visit to pay.

D'Artagnan was well known to the honourable company of king's musketeers, amongst whom it was understood that he would one day take his place; he was therefore regarded as a comrade by anticipation. The result was that the twelve musketeers who had been summoned willingly engaged in the affair to which they had been invited; besides they had the probability of doing an ill turn to the cardinal or his people; and for such expeditions these worthy gentlemen were always well prepared.

Athos divided them into three parties: of one he took the command himself; the second he gave to Aramis; and the third to Porthos; and then each party placed itself in ambush opposite an entrance to the palace.

D'Artagnan, on his part, boldly entered by the principal gate. He gave his letter to the officer on duty, who showed him into the waiting-room, and himself proceeded into the interior of the palace.

In this room there were five of his Eminence's guards, who, recognizing d'Artagnan, and knowing that it was he who had wounded Jussac, looked at him with a singular smile.

This smile seemed to d'Artagnan a bad omen, but he stood boldly before the guards, and waited, with his hand upon his hip, in an attitude not ungraceful.

The officer returned and made a sign to d'Artagnan to follow him. It seemed to the young man that, as he left the room, the guards began to whisper to each other.

He went along a corridor, passed through a large drawing-room, entered a library, and found himself before a man, who was seated at a desk, writing.

The officer introduced him, and retired without uttering a word. D'Artagnan remained standing, and examined this man.

At first he thought he was in the presence of a judge who was examining his papers; but he soon saw that the man at the desk was writing, or rather correcting, lines of unequal length, and was scanning the words upon his fingers; he saw that he was in the presence of a poet. At the expiration of a minute the poet closed his manuscript, on the back of which was written, *Mirame; a Tragedy in Five Acts.*

He raised his head and d'Artagnan recognized the cardinal.

Richelieu rested his elbow on his manuscript, and his cheek on his hand, and looked at d'Artagnan for an instant. No one had an eye more profoundly penetrating than the cardinal; and the young man felt his gaze running through his veins like a fever.

"Sir," said the cardinal, "you are one d'Artagnan, of Béarn?

"Yes, my lord."

"There are several branches of d'Artagnans in Tarbes and in its neighbourhood: to which of them do you belong?"

"I am the son of the one who fought in the religious wars with the great King Henry, the father of his gracious Majesty."

"That is it: it is you who set out from your native place, about seven or eight months ago, to come and seek your fortune in the capital?"

"Yes, my lord."

"You came by Meung, where something happened to you—I do not know exactly what—but something?"

"My lord," said d'Artagnan, "this is what happened—"

"No matter, no matter," interrupted the cardinal with a smile which indicated that he knew the story quite as well as he who wished to narrate it. And he then revealed to d'Artagnan that he knew all about his movements—even his visit to England and being received by the queen on his return.

"On the next day, you were waited upon by Cavois," continued the cardinal: "he came to beg you to come to the palace. But you did not make that visit; and you were wrong."

"My lord, I feared that I had incurred your Eminence's displeasure."

"And why so, sir? Because you had performed the orders of your superiors with more intelligence and courage than another could have done? Incur my displeasure when you merited praise! It is those who do not obey that I punish; and not those who, like you, obey—too well. And to prove it, recall the date of the day on which I sent for you to come to see me, and search your memory for what happened that very night."

It was the evening on which Madame Bonacieux was carried off. D'Artagnan shuddered; and he remembered that, half an hour before this present moment, the poor woman had passed before him, no doubt again borne away by the same power which had directed that first abduction.

"In short," continued the cardinal, "as I have heard nothing of you for some time, I wished to know what you were doing. Besides, you certainly owe me some thanks: you have yourself remarked what consideration has always been shown towards you."

D'Artagnan bowed respectfully.

"That," continued the cardinal, "proceeded not only from a sentiment of natural justice, but also from a plan that I had made respecting you."

D'Artagnan was more and more astonished.

"It was my desire," continued the cardinal, "to explain this plan to you on the day that you received my first invitation; but you did not come. Fortunately, nothing has been lost by the delay; and today you shall hear the explanation. Sit down, then, M. d'Artagnan: you are gentleman enough not to be kept standing whilst you listen." He pointed to a chair. "You are brave, M. d'Artagnan," resumed his Eminence; "and you are prudent, which is far better. I love men of head and heart. Do not be alarmed," he added, smiling; "by men of heart I mean courageous men. But, young as you are, and only on the threshold of the world, your enemies are very powerful. If you do not take care, they will destroy you."

"Alas, my lord!" replied the young man. "They will undoubtedly accomplish it very easily; for they are strong and well supported, whilst I stand alone."

"Come, what would you say to an ensign's commission in my guards, and a company at the end of the campaign?"

"Ah, my lord!"

"You accept it, do you not?"

"My lord—" began d'Artagnan, with an embarrassed air.

"What! Do you decline?" exclaimed the cardinal, with a look of astonishment.

"I am in his Majesty's guards, my lord, and I have no cause to be discontented."

"But it seems to me," said his Eminence, "that my guards are also his Majesty's guards; and that whosoever serves in a French regiment, serves the king."

"My lord, your Eminence has misunderstood my words."

Richelieu then warned d'Artagnan he had received serious complaints against him. D'Artagnan replied that all his friends were among the king's guards, but his enemies in those of his Eminence. But he undertook to fight well in the coming campaign at the siege of La Rochelle in order to earn the cardinal's approval.

"That is to say, you refuse to serve me, sir," declared Richelieu in a tone of mingled vexation and esteem. "I am not offended with you, but you must understand it is enough to protect and recompense one's friends: one owes nothing to one s enemies. And yet I will give you one piece of advice. Take care of yourself, M. d'Artagnan; for from the moment that I withdraw my hand from you, I would not give a farthing for your life."

"I will do my best, my lord," replied the Gascon, with modest confidence.

"And hereafter, at the moment that any misfortune may befall you, remember," said Richelieu pointedly, "that it is I who came to seek you and that I have done what I could to avert that misfortune from you."

"Let what may happen," said d'Artagnan, bowing, with his hand upon his breast, "I shall retain a sentiment of eternal gratitude to your Eminence, for what you are now doing for me."

"Well then, M. d'Artagnan, as you say, we shall see each other again after the campaign. I shall keep my eye upon you, for I shall be there," continued the cardinal, pointing to a magnificent suit of armour, which he was to wear. "And on our return, we will settle our account."

"Ah, my lord!" exclaimed d'Artagnan, "spare me the weight of your displeasure: remain neutral, my lord, if you find that I behave gallantly."

"Young man," said Richelieu, "if I can once more say to you what I have said today, I promise, you that I *will* say it."

This last expression of Richelieu's conveyed a terrible doubt. It alarmed d'Artagnan more than a threat would have done; for it was a warning: it implied that the cardinal was endeavouring to shield him from some impending evil. He opened his lips to answer; but with a haughty gesture, the cardinal dismissed him.

D'Artagnan found Athos and the four musketeers awaiting him at the door, and beginning to be anxious about him. With a word he reassured them, and Planchet ran to the other posts to announce that longer guard was unnecessary, for his master had returned, safe and sound, from the cardinal's palace.

When they reached Athos's apartment, Aramis and Porthos inquired about the object of this singular interview: but d'Artagnan merely told them that Richelieu had sent for him to offer him an ensign's commission in the guards, and that he had refused it.

"And you were right!" exclaimed Aramis and Porthos with one voice. Athos fell into a profound reverie, and said nothing. But, when he was alone with d'Artagnan, he said:

"You have done your duty, but, perhaps, you were imprudent."

The next day was occupied in preparations for departure.

D'Artagnan went to take leave of M. de Tréville. At this time, it was still believed that the separation of the guards and musketeers would be but temporary—as the king was holding his parliament that very day, and proposing to set out on the next. M. de Tréville therefore, only asked d'Artagnan whether he could do anything for him; but d'Artagnan replied that he had all that he needed.

The next day, at the first sound of the trumpets, the friends separated: the musketeers hastened to M. de Tréville's and the guards to M. des Essarts'. Each captain then led his company to the Louvre, where the king reviewed them. His Majesty was sad and seemed in ill-health, which detracted somewhat from his usual dignified appearance.

The review being ended, the guards alone began their march—the musketeers waiting for the king—a delay which gave Porthos an opportunity of displaying his superb equipage to Madame Coquenard, the solicitor's wife.

Aramis, on his part, wrote a long letter. To whom? None knew. In the next room, Kitty, who was to set off that very evening for Tours, was waiting for this mysterious epistle.

Athos drank, sip by sip, the last bottle of his Spanish wine.

In the meantime, d'Artagnan was marching with his company. In passing through the Faubourg St. Antoine, he turned, and looked gaily at the Bastille, which at least as yet he had escaped. As he looked only at the Bastille, he did not see my lady, who, mounted on a dun horse, pointed him out with her finger to two villainous-looking men, who immediately came close up to the ranks to identify him. To a questioning look which they addressed to the lady she answered by a sign that it was he. Then, certain that there could be no mistake in the execution of her orders, she spurred her horse and disappeared.

The two men followed the company; and at the end of the Faubourg St. Antoine, they mounted two horses, which a servant out of livery was holding in readiness for them.

10

The Siege of Rochelle

The siege of La Rochelle was one of the great events of the reign of Louis XIII. Of the important cities which had been given by Henry IV to the Huguenots as places of safety, La Rochelle alone remained. The cardinal wished to destroy this last bulwark of Calvinism.

La Rochelle, which had derived additional importance from the ruin of the other Calvinist towns, was, besides, the last port which remained open to the English in the kingdom of France; and by closing it to England—our eternal enemy—the cardinal would complete the work of Joan of Arc, and the Duke of Guise.

But, alongside these views of his Eminence, which belong to history, we are obliged to dwell upon the petty objects of the lover and the jealous rival.

Richelieu, as everyone knows, had been enamoured of the queen. Was this love a purely political affair, or was it one of those profound passions which Anne of Austria inspired in those around her? We cannot tell. Yet Buckingham had got an advantage over him and in two or three points, especially in the affair of the diamond studs—thanks to the devotion of the three musketeers, and the courage of d'Artagnan—he had cruelly fooled him. Richelieu's object therefore was not merely to rid France of an enemy but to revenge himself on a rival.

Richelieu knew that, in fighting against England, he was fighting against Buckingham; that, in triumphing over England, he should triumph over Buckingham; and lastly, that in humiliating

England in the eyes of Europe, he should humiliate Buckingham in the eyes of the queen.

On his part, Buckingham was impelled by interests absolutely similar to those of the cardinal.

The Duke of Buckingham had gained the first advantage. Arriving unexpectedly before the Isle of Ré, with ninety vessels and twenty thousand men, he had surprised the Count de Toiras, who was the king's commander in the island, and, after a bloody contest, had effected a landing

The Count de Toiras retreated into the citadel of St. Martin with his garrison, and threw a hundred men into a small fort, which was called the fort of La Prée.

This event hastened the decision of the cardinal; and until he and the king could go and take the command of the siege of La Rochelle, which was resolved on, he had sent his Majesty's brother on to direct the first operations, and had made all the troops he could dispose of march towards the theatre of war.

It was to this vanguard that our friend d'Artagnan belonged. The king was to follow when his côurt of justice had been held. But on rising from this sitting on the twenty-eighth of June, he had found himself seized with fever. He had, nevertheless, persisted in setting out; but he grew worse, and was obliged to stop at Villeroi.

Now where the king stopped, there also stopped the musketeers. Hence it followed that d'Artagnan, who was only in the guards, found himself separated, for a time at least, from his good friends, Athos, Porthos and Aramis. This separation, which was only annoying to him, would certainly have become a source of serious anxiety, had he been able to discern by what unsuspected dangers he was surrounded.

He had made an enemy of the cardinal, before whom the nobles of the kingdom trembled; that man had the power to crush him and yet had not done it. And then he had made another enemy—not so much to be feared, he thought, but nevertheless one whom he felt instinctively was not to be despised. That enemy was her ladyship.

Nevertheless, he arrived without mishap at the camp before La Rochelle.

Everything was unchanged. The Duke of Buckingham and his English, in possession of the Isle of Ré, continued to besiege, but without success, the fort of La Prée and the citadel of St. Martin; and the hostilities with La Rochelle had commenced two or three days before, about a fort which the Duke of Angoulême had just constructed near the city.

The guards, under M. des Essarts, were stationed at the Minimes.

D'Artagnan was walking along a pretty path which led from the camp to an adjoining village, when, by the last ray of the setting sun, he thought he saw the barrel of a musket glittering behind a hedge. On the other side of the road, behind a rock, he perceived the muzzle of a second musket. It was evidently an ambuscade.

The young man gave a glance at the first musket, and as soon as he saw the orifice of the barrel motionless, he threw himself upon his face. He heard a ball whistle over his head. He leapt up with a bound, and, at the same moment, the bullet of the second musket scattered the stones in the very part of the path where he had thrown himself down. He immediately ran towards the camp but, fast as was his course, the one who had fired first, having had time to reload, fired another shot at him, so well aimed this time that the ball passed through his hat and carried it ten paces in front of him.

As d'Artagnan had no other hat, he picked it up as he ran; and reaching his quarters, pale and out of breath, he sat down, without speaking to anyone, and began to reflect.

This event might have three causes. The first, and most natural was, that it might be an ambuscade from La Rochelle; or it might be a kind remembrance of the cardinal's; or it might be her ladyship's revenge. This last conjecture was the most probable.

He tried in vain to recall either the features or the dress of the assassins; but he had run away too rapidly to have leisure to notice them.

"Ah, my poor friends," muttered d'Artagnan, "where are you? How much I need you!"

At nine o'clock on the next morning, they beat to arms. The Duke of Orléans was visiting the pickets. The guards mustered, and d'Artagnan took his place amidst his comrades.

After a short time d'Artagnan perceived M. des Essarts making a sign to him to draw near. The Duke of Orléans wanted volunteers for a particularly dangerous expedition, and M. des Essarts had recommended d'Artagnan. He accepted with alacrity, and two guards and two other soldiers joined him.

It was not known whether the Rochellois, after having taken a bastion during the night, had evacuated it, or placed a garrison in it. It was therefore necessary to examine the spot from a point sufficiently near to ascertain this fact.

D'Artagnan went off with his four companions, following the line of the trench. The two guards marched by his side and the soldiers in the rear. Sheltering themselves in this manner by the rampart, they arrived within a hundred paces of the bastion; and turning round at this point, d'Artagnan perceived that the two soldiers had disappeared. Believing them to have remained behind from fear, he continued to advance.

At the turn of the counterscarp they found themselves about sixty yards from the bastion; but they saw no one and the bastion seemed evacuated. The three volunteers deliberated whether they should advance farther, when suddenly a circle of smoke appeared, and a dozen balls whistled around d'Artagnan and his companions.

They knew now what they had come to learn: the bastion was guarded; a longer delay, therefore, in this dangerous place would have been only an unnecessary imprudence. So d'Artagnan and the two guards turned and began a rapid retreat. On reaching the angle of the trench, which would serve them as a rampart, one of the guards fell with a ball through his chest, whilst the other, who was safe, continued his way to camp.

D'Artagnan would not abandon a companion, and leaned over

him to lift him up and aid him to regain the lines; but at that very moment two shots were fired from the rear; one ball shattered the head of the wounded man, and the other was flattened against a rock after having passed within two inches of d'Artagnan's body

The young man turned quickly, remembering the two soldiers who had abandoned him, who now made him recollect his assassins of the previous evening. He fell forward on to the wounded man's body as if he were dead and immediately saw that two heads were raised above an abandoned breastwork, about thirty yards from him: they were those of the two soldiers. They approached with unloaded muskets. When they were about three paces from him, d'Artagnan, who had taken especial care, in falling, not to relinquish his sword, suddenly rose and sprang upon them.

The assassins tried to escape to the enemy. One was shot in the shoulder by the Rochellois; d'Artagnan soon had the point of his sword at the throat of the other.

"Oh, do not kill me!" exclaimed the bandit. "Pardon, sir, and I will confess everything!"

"Wretch!" cried d'Artagnan; "speak quickly. Who engaged you to assassinate me?"

"A woman whom I do not know, but who was called "my lady"."

"But if you do not know this woman, how came you to know her name?"

"My comrade knew her and called her so: it was with him that she made the bargain—not with me. He has a letter from her now in his pocket, which would be of great importance to you, according to what I heard him say."

"But how did you become his partner in this ambuscade?"

"He proposed to me to join him in it, and I agreed."

"And how much has she paid you for this pretty expedition?"

"A hundred louis."

"Well, upon my word," said the young man, laughing, "she thinks me of some value! A hundred louis! It is quite a fortune for two wretches like you. I can well understand that you would accept it; and so I pardon you, but on one condition."

"What is that?" said the soldier, uneasy at discovering that all was not yet ended.

"That you go and get me the letter out of your companion's pocket."

The bandit set off towards his wounded companion, but stopped short, terrified. So d'Artagnan himself crawled to the wounded man and lifted his body up as a protection for himself. Another shot from the Rochellois kil'ed this assassin. In the trench d'Artagnan searched the body and found the following letter:

> Since you have lost track of that woman, and she is now in safety in the convent, which you never ought to have allowed her to reach, take care, at least, not to miss the man; otherwise, you know that I have a long arm, and you shall pay dearly for that hundred louis that you have had of mine.

There was no signature. Nevertheless, it was evident that the letter was from her ladyship. He kept it, therefore, as evidence against her; and finding himself in safety behind the angle of the trench, he began to question the wounded man. The latter confessed that he had been engaged with his comrade, the same who had now been killed, to carry off a young woman, who was to leave Paris by the gate of La Villette; but that having stopped to drink at a wine shop, they had been ten minutes too late for the carriage. They were to have taken her to her ladyship.

D'Artagnan learned with joy that the queen had at last discovered the prison to which poor Madame Bonacieux had been sent to expiate her devotion, and had already rescued her from it. Thus the letter which he had received from the young woman and her appearance in the carriage on the Chaillot road, were explained. He was so happy he pardoned the bandit.

The guard, who had returned at the first discharge from the bastion, had announced the death of his four companions. There was, therefore, both great astonishment and great joy in the regiment, when they saw the young man returning safe and sound.

D'Artagnan explained the sword wound of his companion by a sortie, which he invented. He recounted the death of the other soldier and the perils they had run. This account was the occasion of a veritable triumph. For one day the whole army talked of this expedition; and his Royal Highness himself sent to compliment d'Artagnan on his conduct.

D'Artagnan now thought he might cease to be disturbed; but this tranquillity proved one thing: that he did not yet properly estimate her ladyship.

Little activity took place while the king was recovering from his malady and preparing to set out for La Rochelle as soon as he could. Everyone waited for his arrival to begin operations.

Meanwhile one anxiety still remained in d'Artagnan's mind, which was that he received no tidings of his friends.

But one morning he received an explanation, in the following letter, addressed from Villeroi:

> M. d'Artagnan.
> Messrs. Athos, Porthos and Aramis, after having had a capital
> dinner party at my house, and enjoying themselves very much,
> made so great a noise that the provost of the castle, who is a
> strict disciplinarian, put them in confinement for a few days. I
> must, nevertheless, execute the orders that they gave me, to
> send you a dozen bottles of my Anjou wine, which they
> greatly admired. They hope that you will drink to their healths
> in their own favourite wine.
> I have done this; and am, sir, with great respect, your most
> obedient, humble servant,
>
> Godeau,
> Steward of the Musketeers.

"Good!" exclaimed d'Artagnan. "They think of me amongst their pleasures, as I have thought of them in my troubles. Certainly, I will drink to them, and with all my heart, too; but not alone."

He hastened to invite two other guards. Planchet invited as his helpers the valet of one of the guests and Brisemont, the robber who had tried to murder d'Artagnan, but who now followed him devotedly. The party took place two days later, but just as they sat down and had given the dregs to Brisemont to strengthen him, for he was still very weak, guns announced the arrival of the king. They all rushed out and d'Artagnan was delighted to see Athos, Porthos and Aramis. When he began to thank them for the wine, the three friends denied having sent him any, so in fear they rushed to the guards' mess where the party was being held, to find Brisemont dying of poison and the frightened servants trying to aid him.

"You see! my friends," said d'Artagnan, "it is war to the death. There is no doubt that this is the work of my lady. What is to be done?"

On the advice of Athos, they decided to try to meet her and call a truce to this feud, while Aramis promised to find out through his friend at Tours some news of Constance Bonacieux in her convent.

On this the four friends separated, with the promise of meeting again the same evening.

The arrival of the king, and with him the cardinal, caused great activity. The Isle of Ré was attacked and the English were driven out. But for the musketeers who had not much to do with the siege it was a time of inactivity, and owing to their friendship with M. de Tréville, Athos, Porthos and Aramis obtained much more freedom even than the others. One evening, returning from a visit to the Red Dovecot tavern and suspicious of an ambuscade, they challenged two horsemen who were by themselves. To their amazement, they found these horsemen were the cardinal himself and his equerry. At Richelieu's request, they promised not to say they had seen him, for he did not want it known that he had left the camp. Athos told him they had been in a brawl at the tavern with some drunken wretches who wanted to force the door of a lady staying there. They had not seen her but knew she had a cavalier with her. The cardinal said he had learned what he had left the camp to find out and bade the three friends accompany him. The tavern had been purposely emptied of visitors and while the cardinal and his equerry went upstairs the three friends waited below in a room with a new stone chimney.

It was evident that, without suspecting it, our three friends had rendered a service to someone whom the cardinal honoured with his special protection. But they did not know who it could be. While Porthos and Aramis settled down to a game of dice, Athos paced up and down. Suddenly he realized that through the stove-pipe of the new chimney he could hear everything that the cardinal was saying in the room above.

"Listen, my lady," said the cardinal. "The business is important. Sit down and let us talk."

"My lady!" muttered Athos.

"I am listening to your Eminence with the greatest attention," replied a voice which made him start.

"A small vessel with an English crew, whose captain is devoted to me, awaits you at the mouth of the Charente, at Fort de la Pointe; it will sail tomorrow morning,"

"I must go there tonight, then?"

"Instantly! That is to say, as soon as you have received my instructions. Two men, whom you will find at the door when you go out, will escort you. You will let me leave first, and then half an hour later, you will depart yourself."

"Yes, my lord. Now, let us return to the mission with which you are pleased to charge me; and as I am anxious to continue to merit your confidence, deign to make it plain in clear and precise terms, so that I may not make any error."

Athos took advantage of a pause in the conversation to tell his two companions to fasten the door on the inside, and to beckon them to come and listen with him.

"You will go to London," resumed the cardinal; "on arriving there you will seek out Buckingham."

"I would observe to your Eminence," said her ladyship, "that since the affair of the diamond studs, about which the duke always suspected me, his Grace mistrusts me."

"But you have no need to gain his confidence this time," said the cardinal. "You are to present yourself frankly and loyally, as an ambassadress."

"Frankly and loyally," repeated the lady, with an indescribable accent of duplicity.

"Yes, frankly and loyally," replied the cardinal, in the same tone; "all this business must be transacted openly."

"I will follow your Eminence's instructions to the very letter. I only await your giving them."

"You will go to Buckingham from me and you will tell him that I am aware of all the preparations he is making but that I do not much disturb myself about them, seeing that on the first step he takes, I will destroy the queen."

"Will he believe that your Eminence is in a position to execute your threats?"

"Yes, for I have proofs." Then the cardinal gave her the details.

"But," resumed her ladyship, when the cardinal had proved his point, "if in spite of all these reasons the duke should not surrender, and should continue to menace France—?"

"The duke is in love like a madman, or a ninny," replied Richelieu with intense bitterness. "Like the paladins of old, he has only undertaken this war to obtain a glance from his mistress's eyes. If he knows that the war will cost the lady of his love her honour and perhaps her liberty, I warrant you he will look at it twice."

"But yet," said my lady, with a perseverance which proved that she was determined to understand all that was included in the mission which she was to undertake, "if he persists?"

"If he persists—well, I must put my hope in one of those events which change the fortune of nations."

"If your Eminence would cite to me some of those historical events," said her ladyship, "I might possibly participate in your confidence in the future."

Richelieu then quoted some recent fortunate assassinations. He was certain that some fanatic existed in England who would gladly murder Buckingham, who was loathed by the Puritans. To test her memory, her ladyship recited all that Richelieu had told her, and asked for an order which would ratify any action she might take. Then she asked Richelieu, in turn, for his help against her enemies.

"You have enemies, then?" said Richelieu.

"Yes, my lord, enemies against whom you are bound to support me, since I made them in the service of your Eminence."

"And who are they?" demanded the cardinal.

"There is first, a little busybody, of the name of Bonacieux."

"She is in prison, at Nantes."

"That is to say, she was there," replied my lady; "but the queen has inveigled an order from the king, by which she has removed her to a convent. I do not know where. And your Eminence will let me know in what convent this woman is?

"I see no objection to that," replied the cardinal.

"Very well. Now, I have another enemy, whom I fear far more than this little Madame Bonacieux—her lover." And my lady recounted d'Artagnan's exploits against them both.

"We must first have some proof of his association with the duke," said the cardinal.

"A proof!" exclaimed my lady. "I will find a dozen!"

"Well then, let me have the proof, and it is the simplest thing in the world; I will send him to the Bastille."

"Very well, my lord; but then afterwards?"

"When a man is in the Bastille, there is no *afterwards,*" said the cardinal in a hollow voice. "Give me a pen, ink and paper."

"Here they are, my lord."

"Perfect."

There was a moment's silence which proved that the cardinal was occupied in thinking of the words in which the order should be written, or perhaps writing it. Athos, who had not lost one word of the conversation, took a hand of each of his companions, and led them to the other end of the room. He told them he had heard enough and wanted an excuse to absent himself. In the meantime they were to say he had gone ahead as a scout since he had heard the road was not safe. And he went out.

When he came down, Richelieu had no suspicions; indeed he complimented Porthos and Aramis on Athos's foresight and the party set off. Meanwhile Athos doubled back and returned to the tavern where the landlord recognized him again.

"My officer," said Athos, "has forgotten to give a piece of very important information to the lady on the first floor and has sent me to repair his forgetfulness."

"Go up," said the landlord; "the lady is still in her chamber."

Athos availed himself of this permission, and ascended the stairs with his lightest step; and when he reached the landing, he perceived, through the half-open door, my lady, who was fastening her hat.

He entered the room and closed the door behind him. At the noise he made in bolting it, she turned round. Enveloped in his cloak, and with his hat drawn down over his eyes, Athos was standing upright before the door. On seeing this figure, mute and motionless as a statue, my lady was alarmed.

"Who are you, and what do you want?" she exclaimed.

"Yes, it is certainly she," muttered Athos. Letting his cloak fall and raising his hat, he advanced towards her. Do you recognize me, madame?" said he.

My lady took one step forward, and then recoiled as though she had seen a serpent.

"Come," said Athos, "I can see that you recognize me."

The Count de la Fère!" muttered her ladyship, growing deadly pale and drawing back till the wall prevented her going farther.

"Yes, my lady," replied Athos, "the Count de la Fère in person, who returns expressly from the other world to have the pleasure of seeing you. Let us sit down, then, and talk."

The name of Athos conceals the Count de la Fère, even as the name of Lady de Winter conceals that of Anne de Breuil. Was not that what you were called when your honoured brother married us?" Athos then revealed that he knew all her secrets. "I can recite your actions, day by day, from your entrance into the cardinal's service until tonight," said he. Then he warned her that, whatever she might do to the Duke of Buckingham, if she harmed d'Artagnan, his faithful friend, that crime should be her last.

"He has insulted me; he shall die!" said my lady.

Athos felt his brain begin to reel. He drew his pistol and threatened to blow her brains out if she did not at once give up to him the paper signed by the cardinal. She knew Athos's resolution, and saw he was about to press the trigger. She put her hand into her bosom, pulled out a paper, and Athos, unfolding it, read:

> It is by my order, and for the good of the state, that the bearer
> of this did that which he has now done.
> Richelieu.

"And now," said Athos, resuming his cloak, and replacing his hat, "now that I have drawn your teeth, bite if you can!" He left the room without even once looking behind him.

At the door he found the two men with the led horse.

"Gentlemen," said he, "his lordship's order is, you know, to conduct this woman without loss of time to the Fort de la Pointe, and not to leave her until she is on board."

As these words exactly accorded with the order which they had received, they bowed their heads in token of assent.

Athos sprang lightly into his saddle, and went off at a gallop; only instead of keeping to the road, he went across the fields, halting from time to time to listen for the others. He rejoined the party just before the cardinal and his equerry left them, and received his Eminence's thanks for the care he had taken.

"Well," said Porthos and Aramis, as soon as the cardinal was out of hearing, "he signed the paper she asked for!"

"I know he did," said Athos quietly, "for here it is."

The three friends did not exchange another word before they reached their quarters, except to give the password to the sentinels. But they sent Mousqueton to tell Planchet that his master was requested to come to the musketeers' rooms the instant he left the trenches.

As Athos had foreseen, her ladyship, on finding the two men at the door, followed them without hesitation, realizing that silence was best. Consequently, having travelled all night, she was at Fort de la Pointe by seven in the morning; at eight she had embarked; and at nine the vessel weighed anchor, and made sail for England.

D'Artagnan found his friends gathered together, but their room was no place for a private conversation; the walls were like sheets of paper. They repaired to the Parpaillot inn, but, unfortunately for their purpose, it was full. Falling unwillingly into conversation with the company d'Artagnan began to tell a light-cavalryman, a Swiss, a dragoon and a fourth soldier about the drawing of the Rochellois from the bastion the night before. This led to the point where Athos bet these four a dinner for eight people that he, Porthos, Aramis and d'Artagnan could hold the bastion, which had been left unoccupied, for an hour and have their breakfast there. The bet was accepted, and the four friends set out accompanied by Grimaud, who was full of misgivings. Athos pointed out that the muskets belonging to the casualties of the earlier attack would still be there, so they could go unarmed. But the main reason for this wager was that they might discuss matters there undisturbed, and gain glory for themselves as well. A council in any other place would be observed by the cardinal's spies and their lives would be in danger.

A crowd watched them reach the bastion.

As Athos had foreseen, the bastion was only occupied by about a dozen bodies, French and Rochellois. They collected the muskets and cartridges while Grimaud prepared the breakfast, but Athos would not let them throw the dead bodies into the ditches, saying they might be useful. They found they had twelve muskets and a hundred rounds of ammunition. Grimaud took up duty as sentinel.

"And now to breakfast!" said Athos.

The four friends squatted on the ground with their legs crossed like Turks or tailors.

"As you are no longer afraid of being heard," said d'Artagnan,

"I hope that you are going to let us into your secret."

"I saw her ladyship, last night," said Athos.

"You saw your wi—" demanded d'Artagnan, his hands shaking.

"Hush, these gentlemen are not initiated into the secrets of my family affairs," interrupted Athos.

"Where did that happen?" demanded d'Artagnan.

"About two leagues from hence, at the Red Dovecot."

"In that case, I am a lost man," said d'Artagnan.

"Not just yet," replied Athos; "for, by this time, she must have quitted the shores of France."

D'Artagnan breathed again.

Now they were interrupted by a troop of twenty Rochellois advancing along a trench towards them. The four friends fired with deadly accuracy, killing six men and wounding one other. The rest fled. They dashed out to recover the weapons of the dead men and then returned to resume their conversation.

"You were saying," said d'Artagnan, "that after demanding my head of the cardinal, her ladyship left the shores of France. Where is she going?" he added, painfully anxious about the itinerary of the lady's journey.

"She is going to England," replied Athos.

"What for?"

"To assassinate the Duke of Buckingham, or to get him assassinated."

D'Artagnan uttered an exclamation of surprise and horror. "It is infamous!" exclaimed he.

"Oh, as to that," said Athos, "I beg you to believe that I care very little about it. Now that you have finished, Grimaud, tie a napkin to that pike and fix it on top of our bastion, that those rebellious Rochellois may see that they are opposed to brave and loyal subjects of the king."

Grimaud obeyed without reply; and an instant afterwards the white flag floated over the heads of the four friends.

A thunder of applause saluted its appearance. Half the camp was at the barriers.

"What!" said d'Artagnan. "Do you care so little about her assassinating Buckingham, or causing him to be assassinated? The duke is a friend."

"The duke is an Englishman; the duke is fighting against us: let her do therefore what she likes with the duke. I care as little about him as I care for an empty bottle."

"And this document?" said d'Artagnan. "Did it remain in her hands?"

"No, it passed into mine. I cannot say that it was without some trouble; for if I said that I should tell a lie."

"Then it was to visit her that you quitted us?" said Aramis.

"Exactly so." Athos took the precious paper from the pocket of his coat. D'Artagnan unfolded it with a hand, of which he did not attempt to hide the tremor, and read:

> It is by my order, and for the good of the state, that the bearer of this did that which he has now done.
> Richelieu.

"It is, in fact, a regular absolution," said Aramis.

"We must destroy this paper," said d'Artagnan, who fancied he read in it his own death sentence

"On the contrary," replied Athos, "it must be most scrupulously preserved; and I would not give it up for as many gold coins as would cover it."

They were discussing what to do next and d'Artagnan had just said he had an idea when Grimaud called out to them that a band of twenty to twenty-five soldiers was advancing on them.

"Suppose we return to the camp now?" said Porthos. "It seems to me that the match is not equal."

"Impossible for three reasons," answered Athos. "The first is because we have not finished our breakfast. The second because we still have some important affairs to talk about; and the third, it wants yet ten minutes before the hour is elapsed."

"All the same," said Aramis, "we must arrange a plan of battle."

"It is vastly simple," replied Athos. "As soon as the enemy is within musket-shot, we must fire; in fact, we must blaze away as long as we have guns loaded. If the remnant of the band should then wish to mount to the assault, we must let the besiegers reach the ditch, and then we must heave down on their heads a large mass of the wall, which only stays up now by a miracle of equilibrium."

The four guns made but one report, and four men fell.

The drum then beat, and the little band advanced at the double.

At three other reports, two men fell; yet the march of those who remained unwounded did not slacken.

When they reached the foot of the bastion, twelve or fifteen of the enemy remained. A last discharge delayed but did not stop them. They leapt into the ditch and prepared to scale the breach.

"Now, my friends," said Athos, "let us finish them at one blow. To the wall! To the wall!"

And the four friends, assisted by Grimaud, set themselves to topple with the barrels of their muskets an enormous mass of wall, which bowed as though the wind swayed it, and, loosening itself from its base, fell with a tremendous crash into the ditch. A fearful cry was then heard; a cloud of dust ascended towards the sky; and—that was all.

Three or four unfortunate beings, covered with mire and blood, fled along the hollow way and regained the town. They were all the survivors of the little band.

Athos looked at his watch. "Gentlemen," he said, "we have been here an hour, and now the wager is gained: but we must be fair players; besides, d'Artagnan has not yet told us his idea." And the musketeer, with his habitual coolness, seated himself at the remains of the breakfast.

D'Artagnan suggested he should go to London once more and warn Buckingham. The others said this would be treason as they were now at war. Porthos suggested that as he was unknown to my lady he should go and strangle her. Aramis said no, they could not kill a woman, and what they should do was to inform the queen. He undertook to send a letter safely to her, through a clever friend at Tours. And they would also inform Lord de Winter who, they knew, was now in London.

By now a large army of Rochellois was advancing, so they decided to leave. They brought in the napkin-banner and three holes were shot through it when Athos waved it at the enemy. The dead bodies were propped up by Grimaud to look like live soldiers. This delayed the Rochellois as they feared an ambush, but they re-occupied the bastion just before the four friends got out of range. Bullets were actually flattened on the stones around them, and the fusillade continued, but they were soon beyond its range.

They received a tumultuous welcome from the two thousand persons in the camp who had witnessed the incident. The light-horseman and the other wagerers hastened to confess they had lost their bet.

Even the cardinal was pleased when he heard of it and ordered d'Artagnan to be promoted a musketeer. D'Artagnan could not contain himself for joy. His last request to M. des Essarts was to change the queen's ring for money—they had decided to send their servants with the letters to the Queen and Lord de Winter, as they themselves could not leave the camp, and they needed something to cover their expenses. M. des Essarts was able to give d'Artagnan seven thousand livres in gold.

The breakfast at M. de Tréville's, to celebrate d'Artagnan's promotion, was charmingly gay. D'Artagnan had already got his uniform. He was about the same size as Aramis; and as Aramis had been so handsomely paid by the bookseller who had bought his poem, he had furnished himself with two of everything and so he provided his friend with a complete equipment.

D'Artagnan would have been completely happy, had he not seen her ladyship like a dark cloud on the horizon.

After breakfast they agreed to meet again in the evening at Athos's quarters, in order to make their final arrangements. D'Artagnan passed the day in displaying his musketeer's uniform in every avenue throughout the camp.

At the appointed time in the evening, the four friends assembled. There were only three things left to decide: what they should write to my lady's brother-in-law; what they should write to Aramis's friend at Tours; and which of the valets should be the bearers of the letters.

After long argument, it was decided that Aramis should write the letters; that Bazin should carry the letter to Tours; and Planchet the letter to London.

The letters penned by Aramis received his friends' enthusiastic approval. Mounted on an excellent horse, which he was to leave twenty leagues from La Rochelle to take the post, and carrying one thousand four hundred of d'Artagnan's livres, Planchet went off at a gallop. He was given sixteen days to complete his commission. As he was leaving d'Artagnan had taken him aside and added: "When you have given the letter to Lord de Winter and he has read it, you will say to him "Watch over Lord Buckingham for there is a plot to assassinate him." This is so serious and important that I will not write it."

Bazin left the next morning for Tours, and had eight days and six hundred livres allowed him for his expedition.

The four friends, during the whole time of their valets' absence, had, as may be well supposed, their eyes and ears more than ever on the alert. The days were spent in trying to catch every report, to watch the movements of the cardinal, and to scent out the couriers who arrived. More than once an unconquerable anxiety seized them, on being sent for on some unexpected service. They had also to be watchful of their own safety; her ladyship was a phantom who, having once appeared to anyone, would nevermore allow him to sleep in tranquillity.

On the morning of the eighth day, Bazin, fresh as ever and smiling as usual, entered the room at the Parpaillot, just as the four friends were sitting down to breakfast, saying, according to the agreement they had made:

"Monsieur Aramis, here is the answer from your cousin."

Aramis read out the letter:

> Cousin,
> My sister and I understand dreams very well, and we even
> have a shocking fear of them: but of yours it may be said, I
> hope—all dreams are false! Adieu! Take care of yourself, and
> let us hear of you from time to time.

But Planchet did not come. Then, on the sixteenth evening, just as he was despaired of, he appeared as the friends were leaving the Parpaillot, and handed a note to d'Artagnan. Back at camp, they opened it. In true British brevity, it merely said:

> Thank you: be easy.

And in a few days they received another letter from Aramis's friend at Tours, telling them that Madame Bonacieux was detained in a convent at Béthune, in northern France.

11

A Vile Plot

In the meantime, her ladyship—intoxicated with rage and pacing up and down the vessel's deck like an excited lioness—was crossing to England. The ship had tacked about continually thanks to a continuing wind and rough seas and the presence of English and French cruisers, and it was not till the very day that Planchet embarked at Portsmouth for France that her ship entered the roadstead. The town of Portsmouth was in a state of extraordinary excitement. Four large ships, recently built, had just been launched. Standing on the jetty, Buckingham was visible, surrounded by a staff almost as gorgeous as himself.

As they were preparing to cast anchor, a cutter approached with an officer and eight men in it. The officer came on board and examined all the passengers. He was about twenty-five, pale, with deep-set blue eyes. He had a fine mouth in a chestnut-coloured beard and a strong chin which showed obstinacy, with short, thin hair shading his slightly receding forehead. His expression was perfectly motionless and impenetrable. He stopped in front of her ladyship and studied her with great care but without addressing a word to her. As the ship approached the quay he took her and her luggage off, saying it was a wartime precaution. She was put into a carriage, and not until she saw that they were leaving Portsmouth did she protest. But the officer remained immovable to her threats and cries, and when they arrived at a gloomy, massive castle, she was shown into a room, where he told her that a certain person had ordered him to arrest her at sea and bring her to this castle. That person was coming to see her.

She was astounded when Lord de Winter, her brother-in-law, appeared. He turned to the officer and said:

"It is all right, I thank you. Now leave us, Mr. Felton."

But try as he would, Lord de Winter could elicit no information from his sister-in-law, who maintained that she had come to England purely to see him. He told her that, where she now was, they would see each other every day and that she could have the same luxuries that her first—French—husband, gave her. As he was still alive they could find out from him what they were. My lady foamed with rage, and sprang towards him, but he awaited her attack with composure, saying he knew that she was in the habit of assassinating people, and that his would not be the first man's hand to be laid upon her. And he pointed accusingly to her left shoulder. He told her that he realized she was his only heir and had come to secure his money, but that he had taken precautions now and made other arrangements for it even if she were to succeed in killing him. If she were not his brother's wife, he would have had her imprisoned or executed but, as it was, she was to be closely guarded, and when he sailed for La Rochelle she would be taken to a southern colony with a companion who would blow her brains out at the first attempt she might make to return to Britain or the Continent. Felton was called in to swear to carry out loyally all Lord de Winter's commands. There was no acting in the way the young officer looked at her ladyship with loathing in his open face.

Yet, in five days, using every wile known to woman, and accusing Buckingham as the cunning contriver of her ruin, she succeeded in melting Felton's heart. Overcome with love, he brought a knife at her request, to be left with her. But Lord de Winter entered unexpectedly, and jeeringly declared that she would never dare to kill herself. My lady, feeling that all would be lost unless she could give Felton an immediate proof of her courage, stabbed herself. Felton snatched the knife away, but it had fortunately—or perhaps, skilfully—encountered the steel busk which at that period defended women's bosoms. It had glided down it and penetrated slanting between the flesh and the ribs. My lady's dress was thereupon stained with blood in a second, and she fell back apparently insensible.

"See, my lord," said Felton with a gloomy look, "this woman, who was under my guard, has slain herself."

"Do not worry, Felton," replied Lord de Winter; "she is not dead: demons do not die so simply. Do not worry, but go and wait for me in my apartments."

At this order from his superior Felton obeyed; but as he went out he put the knife in his bosom.

Lord de Winter, meantime, contented himself with summoning the woman who waited upon her ladyship, and as the wound might, after all, be really serious, he immediately dispatched a man on horseback for a surgeon.

On learning that the wound was not serious, Lord de Winter visited his sister-in-law to tell her he was getting an immediate order from Buckingham for her banishment. At midday, next day, 23rd August, she would be sent away under a heavy guard. Meantime he had changed her guard and sent Felton away.

This was the final blow. Felton was mistrusted! She was alone, despairing of her fate, when suddenly she heard a tap at the window. A man's face appeared behind the bars. "Felton!" she cried. "I am saved!"

"Yes," said Felton, "but be silent!"

He spent the next hour filing through the bars. At the end of this time her ladyship climbed on to a chair, Felton fastened her wrists together with a handkerchief and tied a cord over it, she put her arms round his neck and let herself slip out of the window. He then descended a rope ladder slowly, remaining motionless while the guard patrol passed beneath them.

The castle was close to the shore, and Felton led the way to a small boat in which they were rowed to a sloop where Felton ordered the captain to take her ladyship to France. But first, they

were to heave-to in Chichester Bay, so that Felton could obey
Lord de Winter's orders and go to Buckingham for the warrant
banishing Lady de Winter. The sloop was to wait for him until
ten o'clock; otherwise she was to sail and he would rejoin her
ladyship at the convent at Béthune.

Felton took leave of her ladyship and hastened to Portsmouth,
where he found the whole population astir. The drums were beating in the streets and in the harbour; and the troops about to be
embarked were descending towards the sea. Felton arrived at the
Admiralty House, covered with dust and soaking with perspiration.

"An express from Lord de Winter," said he.

At the name of Lord de Winter, who was known to be one of
Buckingham's most intimate friends, the officer gave an order to
admit Felton, who, after all, wore a naval officer's uniform himself.

Felton darted into the house, but the moment he reached the
hall, another man also entered, covered with dust and out of
breath, having left at the gate a posthorse, which, on reaching it,
had sunk on to its knees. Felton and he addressed Patrick, the
duke's confidential valet, at the same moment. Felton gave Lord
de Winter's name. The stranger would give no name, insisting he
could declare himself to the duke alone and on being allowed
priority of admission. Patrick, who knew that Lord de Winter
was connected, both by profession and friendship, with his
Grace, gave the preference to him who came in his name. The
other was obliged to wait, and it was easy enough to see how
heartily he cursed the delay.

The valet conducted Felton through a large room, in which
were waiting the deputies from La Rochelle, headed by the
Prince de Soubise, and introduced him into a closet where Buckingham, just out of the bath, was finishing his toilet, to which,
now, as ever, he accorded extreme attention. On Patrick's appearance he put on a blue velvet doublet.

"Lieutenant Felton," said Patrick, "from Lord de Winter."

"From Lord de Winter?" repeated Buckingham. "Show him in."

Felton entered.

"Why did not the baron come himself?" asked Buckingham.

"He has a lady prisoner at his castle, and it is about that prisoner that I wish to speak to your Grace," replied Felton.

"Well, proceed."

"What I have to say to you, my lord, must be heard by yourself alone."

"Leave us, Patrick," said Buckingham, "but keep within sound of the bell; I will call you presently."

Patrick left the room.

"We are alone, sir," said Buckingham. "Speak."

"My lord," replied Felton, "the Baron de Winter lately wrote to your Grace requesting you to sign an order for the transportation of a young woman, named Charlotte Backson."

"Yes, sir; and I replied that he should either bring or send me the order, and I would sign it."

"Here it is, my lord."

"Give it to me," said the duke.

Taking the paper from Felton's hands, his Grace cast a rapid glance over its contents. Then, perceiving it was really that which had been referred to, he laid it on the table, took a pen, and prepared to sign it.

"Pardon me, my lord," said Felton, interrupting him, "but is your Grace aware that Charlotte Backson is not this young woman's real name?"

"Yes, sir, I know that," replied the duke, dipping his pen in the ink.

"Then your Grace is acquainted with her real name?" demanded Felton in an abrupt tone.

"I do know it."

The duke put the pen to the paper. Felton grew pale.

"And knowing this real name," resumed Felton, "will your Grace still sign the paper?"

"Certainly," said Buckingham, "and rather twice than once."

"I cannot believe," continued Felton, in a voice which became more and more abrupt and reproachful, "that your Grace is aware that this refers to Lady de Winter."

"I know it, though I am astonished that you know it." And Buckingham refused to withhold his signature.

Felton, throwing himself between the duke and the bell, became more and more excited. "Beware, my lord," he cried threateningly, God will punish you hereafter, but I will punish you here!"

"This is too much!" cried Buckingham, taking a step towards the door.

Felton barred his passage, and holding out a paper to him: "Sign, my lord, sign Lady de Winter's liberation," he cried.

"What! By force? You are joking! Help!" cried the duke, springing for his sword.

But Felton did not give him time to draw it: the open knife with which her ladyship had wounded herself was concealed under his doublet, and in one bound he was upon the duke.

At the same moment Patrick entered the room, exclaiming:

"My lord, a letter from France."

"From France!" cried Buckingham, forgetting everything as he imagined from whom that letter came.

Felton took advantage of the moment, and buried the knife up to its handle in the duke's side.

"Ah, traitor!" exclaimed Buckingham. "Thou hast slain me!"

"Murder!" screamed Patrick.

Felton cast his eyes around for means of escape, and seeing the door free, he rushed into the adjoining room, passed through it still running, and hurried towards the staircase. But upon the first step he met Lord de Winter, who—seeing him wild-looking and livid, and with blood upon his hands and face rushed upon him and exclaimed:

"I knew it! I foresaw it! One minute too late! Oh, how unfortunate is my lot!"

Felton did not attempt to resist, and Lord de Winter handed him over to the guards, who conducted him to a little terrace overlooking the sea until they should receive fresh orders. His lordship himself hastened into Buckingham's room.

On hearing the duke's cry and Patrick's scream, the man whom Felton had met in the antechamber rushed in. He found the duke lying on a sofa, pressing his hand convulsively over the wound.

"La Porte," said the duke, in a dying voice, "La Porte, do you come from her?"

"Yes, your Grace," replied the faithful servant of Anne of Austria, "but I fear I come too late."

"Hush, La Porte, you might be overheard—Patrick let no one enter. Oh, I shall not know what she says to me! My God! I am dying!"

The duke fainted.

In the meantime Lord de Winter, the deputies, the leaders of the expedition, and the officers of Buckingham's household, had already forced their way into the room. Cries of despair resounded on every side. The tidings which had filled the house with lamentations and groans, soon spread, and became generally known throughout the town; whilst the report of a cannon announced that something new and unexpected had happened.

Lord de Winter tore his hair. "One minute too late! Oh, my God, my God! What a misfortune!"

He had, in fact, at seven o'clock in the morning, received information that a rope ladder had been found suspended from one of the windows of the castle; and instantly hastening to her ladyship's chamber, he had found it empty, the window open, and the bars filed through. Remembering then the verbal warning which d'Artagnan had sent to him by his messenger, he had trembled for the duke; and, without a moment's delay, he had galloped at full speed to Portsmouth, where, as we have already said, he encountered Felton on the topmost step.

But Buckingham was not yet dead. He recovered his senses, opened his eyes, and hope revived in all their hearts.

"Gentlemen," said he, "leave me alone with Patrick and La Porte."

There remained in the room only the wounded duke La Porte and Patrick. A surgeon had been summoned but could not be found.

"You will live, my lord, you will live!" repeated Anne of Austria's messenger, kneeling before the duke.

"What has she written to me? Read me the letter," said Buckingham, "read quickly; for I can no longer see!"

La Porte hesitated no longer. The letter was as follows:

> My Lord,
> By all that I have suffered through you and for you, since I
> have known you, I conjure you, if you have deny regard to my
> repose, to put an end to those vast preparations which you are
> making against France, and to relinquish a war, of which it is
> openly said, religion is the avowed, and your love of me, the
> secret, cause. The war may not only bring great calamities on
> France and England, but even upon yourself, my lord—
> misfortunes for which I could never be consoled. Be careful of
> your own life which is threatened, and which will be dear to
> me from the moment when I shall no longer be obliged to
> consider you an enemy.
> Your affectionate Anne.

Buckingham roused all his fast-failing energies to listen to this letter; and when it was ended, as if he had experienced a bitter disappointment—

"Have you nothing more to tell me no—verbal message, La Porte?" demanded he.

"Yes, my lord; the queen charged me to bid you be upon your guard, for she had been warned that you were to be assassinated!"

"And is that all? Is that all?" resumed Buckingham impatiently.

"She charged me also to tell you that she always loved you."

"Ah," said Buckingham, "God be praised! My death, then, will not be to her as the death of a stranger! Patrick," he continued, "bring me the casket in which the diamond studs were kept and the white satin bag on which her initials are embroidered in pearls."

Patrick obeyed.

"Here, La Porte," said Buckingham, "are the only tokens which I have received from her—this silver casket and these two letters. You will restore them to her Majesty; and, for a last souvenir—he looked around him for some precious object—"you will add to them."

He still strove to find some gift; but his eyes, dimmed by death, encountered nothing but the knife which had fallen from Felton's hand, still reeking with blood.

"You will add to them this knife," said the duke, pressing La Porte's hand.

He was just able to place the satin bag in the casket, and to drop the knife upon it, as he made a sign to La Porte that he could no longer speak. Then he slipped from the sofa to the floor.

Patrick uttered a loud cry.

At this moment the duke's surgeon arrived. He approached the duke, took his hand, held it for a moment in his own, and then let it fall again.

"It is all in vain," said he; "he is dead."

"Dead, dead!" echoed Patrick.

As soon as Lord de Winter knew that Buckingham had expired, he ran to Felton, whom the soldiers still guarded on the terrace.

"Wretch," said he to the young man, who, since Buckingham's death, had recovered that tranquillity and coolness which were never more to abandon him, "wretch, what have you done?"

"I have avenged myself!" he replied.

"Yourself!" cried the baron. "Say, rather, that you have been the instrument of that cursed woman; but I swear to you that it shall be her last crime."

"I do not know what you mean," replied Felton calmly, "and I am quite ignorant of what woman you are speaking, my lord. I have killed the Duke of Buckingham, because he twice refused to make me a captain at your request. I have punished him for his injustice—for no other reason."

De Winter, stupified, looked at the men who were binding Felton, and knew not what to think of such insensibility.

Suddenly Felton started. His glance became fixed upon a point on the sea, which the terrace where he stood completely overlooked. With a sailor's eagle eye, he had discovered there, where another could only have seen a speck upon the ocean, the sail of a sloop, which was sailing towards the shores of France. He grew pale, and at once comprehended how he had been betrayed.

"Grant me one last favour?" said he to the baron.

"What is it?" demanded the latter.

"What time is it?"

The baron drew out his watch. "It wants ten minutes to nine," said he.

Her ladyship, then, had anticipated the time of her departure by an hour and a half. As soon as she heard the cannon which announced the fatal event, she had ordered the anchor to be weighed.

Lord de Winter followed his look, observed his suffering, and guessed all.

"Be punished, *alone*, wretch, in the first place," he said to Felton, who allowed himself to be dragged away, with his eyes still turned towards the sea; "but I swear to you, by the memory of my brother, whom I so truly loved, that your accomplice is not saved."

Felton hung down his head without uttering a word.

As for Lord de Winter, he hastily descended the stairs and went to the harbour.

12

A Just Retribution

The first fear of the king of England, Charles I, on hearing of the Duke of Buckingham's death, was that such terrible news might discourage the people of La Rochelle: hence he endeavoured, says Richelieu in his memoirs, to conceal it from them for as long as possible, closing all the ports of his kingdom. But two ships had already left the port; one bearing, as we know, her ladyship. As for the second vessel, we shall hereafter be told whom it carried, and how it got away.

During this time, nothing extraordinary had occurred at the camp before La Rochelle, except that the king, who was, as usual, bored, and perhaps more so at the camp than elsewhere, resolved to go incognito to enjoy the festival of St. Louis at St. Germain, and requested the cardinal to provide for him an escort of twenty musketeers. The cardinal, who sometimes was wearied by the king's gloominess, willingly gave this leave of absence to his royal lieutenant, who promised to return by the fifteenth of September.

When M. de Tréville was informed of this journey by his Eminence, he prepared his baggage; and as, without knowing the cause, he was fully aware of the imperious need that the four friends had for visiting Paris, he marked them out as part of the escort.

Their anxiety to return to Paris was occasioned by the danger which Madame Bonacieux was likely to incur from encountering her mortal enemy, Lady de Winter, at the convent of Béthune. Aramis, therefore, as we have said, had written immediately to that seamstress of Tours who had such exalted acquaintances to solicit from the queen an order empowering Madame Bonacieux to leave the convent, and take refuge either in Lorraine or Belgium. The answer was not long delayed, for in eight or ten days, Aramis had received this letter:

> My dear Cousin,
> Here is my sister's order to withdraw our little servant from the convent of Béthune, where you think the air does not agree with her. My sister sends you this order with great pleasure, for she is much attached to this little girl, whom she hopes to benefit in the end. I embrace you.
> Marie Michon.

To this letter was appended an order in these terms:

> The superior of the convent of Béthune will deliver into the hands of the bearer of this note the novice who entered her convent under my recommendation and patronage.
> Anne.
> At the Louvre, August 10, 1628.

On the night of the 23rd, the escort at length passed through Paris. The king thanked M. de Tréville and allowed him to grant four days' leave of absence to his men, on condition that not one of the favoured individuals should appear at any public place, under penalty of the Bastille.

The first four leaves were granted, as may be imagined, to our four friends; and more than that, Athos persuaded M. de Tréville to extend it to six days instead of four, and managed to cram two more nights into these six days; for they set off on the 24th at 5 o'clock in the evening, and M. de Tréville had as a further kindness post-dated the leave to the morning of the 25th.

On the evening of the 25th, as they were entering Arras, and just as d'Artagnan had dismounted at the tavern of the Golden Harrow to drink a glass of wine, a cavalier came out of the postyard where he had just changed his horse and proceeded at full gallop on the road to Paris. At the moment that he issued from the great gate into the street, the wind opened the cloak in which he was wrapped, although it was the month of August, and lifted up his hat which he caught and pushed violently down upon his forehead.

D'Artagnan, whose eyes were on this man, turned very pale, and let his glass fall. He had recognized the man from Meung.

"Here, sir!" cried a stable boy, running after the stranger. "Here is a paper that fell out of your hat. Hallo, sir! Hallo!"

"Friend," said d'Artagnan, "half a pistole for that paper!"

"Faith, sir, with the greatest pleasure: here it is."

The stable boy, delighted with the good day's work he had done, went back into the yard, and d'Artagnan unfolded the paper.

"Well?" inquired his friends, listening.

"Only one word!" said d'Artagnan.

" "Armentières"," read Porthos. "Armentières? I do not know the place."

"And this name is written in her hand," said Athos.

"Come, come, let us take great care of this paper;' said d'Artagnan; "perhaps I shall not have thrown away my half-pistole. To horse, my friends—to horse!"

The four companions set off at a gallop, on the road to Béthune.

Great criminals are endowed with a kind of predestination which enables them to surmount every obstacle, and to escape every danger until the moment on which a wearied providence has fixed for the shipwreck of their unhallowed fortunes.

Thus it was with her ladyship. She passed between the cruisers of two nations, and landed at Boulogne without mishap, representing herself as a Frenchwoman, whom the English persecuted at Portsmouth on account of the hatred they entertained for France. Her ladyship had, moreover, the best of passports—beauty—aided by the liberality with she scattered her pistoles. She only remained at Boulogne a sufficient time to put into the post a letter written in these terms:

To his Eminence the Lord Cardinal Richelieu, at his camp
before La Rochelle.

My lord, your Eminence may be assured that his Grace the
Duke of Buckingham will not set out for France.

Lady de—
Boulogne, evening of the 25th.

P.S. According to your Eminence's desire, I am proceeding to
the Carmelite convent, Béthune, where I shall await your
orders.

In fact, her ladyship began her journey on the same night.
Darkness overtook her, and she slept at a tavern on the road; at
five o'clock the next morning she resumed her journey, and in
three hours reached Béthune. She inquired her way to the convent of the Carmelites, and went straight there. The abbess came
to meet her, and when her ladyship showed the cardinal's order, a
chamber was immediately prepared for her, and breakfast served.

Her ladyship wished to please the abbess and this was a very
easy task for a woman so truly superior as she was; she endeavoured to be amiable and charmed the good abbess by her varied
conversation, as well as by the graces of her person.

The abbess, who was of a noble family, loved particularly that
gossip of the court which so rarely reaches the extremities of the
kingdom, and which has, above all, so much difficulty in passing
through the walls of a convent, on whose threshold all worldly
sounds cease.

Her ladyship elicited the fact that the sympathies of the abbess
lay with the king and not with the cardinal, so she proclaimed
herself one of his Eminence's victims. The abbess then told her
she had in the convent a young novice, another of the cardinal's
victims, who called herself Kitty. Pretending to be curious to find
out if this was her former maid, her ladyship asked to meet her.
The young woman's face was, of course, unknown to her but
after some time she discovered by skilful questioning that the
young novice was actually Madame Bonacieux, and so she pretended to be overjoyed to meet her. Madame Bonacieux, con-

vinced by her ladyship's show of affection, told her that her friend d'Artagnan, was coming to Béthune to rescue her and imprudently showed her a letter.

> My dear child: Be ready. *Our friend* will see you soon, and
> will see you only to snatch you from the prison where it was
> necessary for your own safety to conceal you. Our charming
> Gascon has just proved himself as brave and faithful as ever.
> Tell him that there is much gratitude to him in a certain quarter
> for the warning he gave.

"Madame de Chevreuse's writing," said my lady to herself. "I was sure messages came from that quarter. Do you know what the warning was?" she asked aloud.

"No, I only suspect he has warned the queen against some new machination of the cardinal."

Madame Bonacieux then left the room on the announcement that a stranger had arrived to see her ladyship. As soon as she had gone, a man appeared; my lady uttered a cry of joy. It was the Count de Rochefort, the intimate friend of his Eminence.

"Ah!" exclaimed both Rochefort and her ladyship at the same instant; "it is you!"

"And you come from—" demanded her ladyship.

"From La Rochelle. And you?"

"From England."

"And Buckingham—"

"Is dead or dangerously wounded. As I was leaving without having obtained anything from him, a fanatic assassinated him."

"Ah!" said Rochefort, smiling; "that was a very fortunate chance, which will please his Eminence much. Have you informed him of it?"

"I wrote to him from Boulogne. But what brings you here?"

"His Eminence was uneasy and sent me to look for you."

"And what have you been doing since?"

"I have not been wasting my time. I have found the mistress of young d'Artagnan: Madame Bonacieux, whose refuge the cardinal could not discover."

"This is a chance quite fit to pair with the other," said Rochefort. "Truly, the cardinal is a fortunate man."

"Fancy my astonishment," continued her ladyship, "when I found myself face to face with this woman."

"Does she know you?"

"No." Her ladyship smiled. "I am her dearest friend."

"Upon my honour," said Rochefort, "my dear countess, it is only you who can perform this sort of miracle."

"And well it is that I can, chevalier," said her ladyship, "for d'Artagnan and his friends are coming for her tomorrow or the next day, with an order from the queen."

"They are going to such a length that we shall be obliged to put them in the Bastille."

"And why has it not been done already?"

"How can I tell? Because the cardinal evinces a weakness toward these men which I cannot comprehend."

"Really! Well then, tell him this, Rochefort: tell him that our conversation at the Red Dovecot was overheard by these men—tell him, that after his departure, one came up and took by force from me the passport he had given me—tell him that they gave Lord de Winter notice of my voyage to England—that this time, again, they nearly prevented the success of my undertaking, as they did in the affair of the diamond studs—tell him, that amongst these four men, only two are to be feared, d'Artagnan and Athos—tell him that the third, Aramis, is Madame de Chevreuse's lover: he must be allowed to live, for his secret is known and he may be made useful—as for the fourth, Porthos, he is a fool, a fop, a ninny, not worth giving oneself the smallest trouble about. What did the cardinal say to you about me?"

"That I must take your despatches, verbal or written. When he knows what you have done, he will give you further instructions."

"I must remain here, then?"

"Here, or in the neighbourhood."

They arranged that Rochefort's carriage, which had broken

down at Lillers, should be sent on for my lady's use, with an order to his servant to place himself at her disposal, that Rochefort should speak harshly of her ladyship to the abbess as one of the cardinal's victims, and that she should wait for him at Armentières on the border. She wrote the name of the village on a slip of paper.

"Good," said Rochefort, taking the paper which he stuffed into the lining of his hat. "And I shall, besides, as a safeguard against the loss of the paper, repeat the name all the way I go. Now, is that all?"

"I think so."

"Let us see—Buckingham dead or grievously wounded—your conversation with the cardinal overheard by the musketeers—Lord de Winter warned of your arrival at Portsmouth—d'Artagnan and Athos to the Bastille—Aramis, Madame de Chevreuse's lover—Porthos a fool—Madame Bonacieux discovered—to send you the carriage as soon as possible—to put my lackey under your orders—to make you out a victim of the cardinal, that the abbess may have no suspicion—Armentières: is that right?"

"My dear chevalier, you are a miracle of memory."

An hour afterwards Rochefort set out at full speed; five hours afterwards he passed through Arras. Our readers already know how he was recognized by d'Artagnan, and how that recognition, by exciting the fears of our four musketeers, had given a new impetus to their journey.

Scarcely had Rochefort left, before Madame Bonacieux returned. She found her ladyship with a smiling countenance, but little guessed the reason.

It was imperative for my lady to get Madame Bonacieux away to a place of safety and there, in case of necessity, use her as a hostage against d'Artagnan. So she deceived her by saying that the letter from Madame de Chevreuse was a forgery and that d'Artagnan would not come, and persuaded the young woman to come away in the carriage with her. Madame Bonacieux was to get into the carriage as if to bid her ladyship farewell and then it was to set off at a gallop. They made quick preparation, but as they were having some food and wine, they heard horsemen. Her ladyship ran to the window and saw eight horsemen, one two lengths in advance of the others. She uttered a stifled groan. In the first horseman she recognized d'Artagnan.

It is the cardinal's guards," she cried. "Let us fly."

But Madame Bonacieux was rooted to the spot in terror.

All at once my lady ran to the table and poured into Madame Bonacieux's glass the contents of a ring which she opened with singular dexterity.

"Drink," she said, "this wine will give you strength."

She put the glass to the lips of the young woman, who drank mechanically. And my lady rushed from the room.

There was a loud murmur of many approaching voices, in the midst of which Madame Bonacieux fancied she heard her own name mentioned. Suddenly she uttered a loud cry of joy, and rushed towards the door—she had recognized d'Artagnan's voice.

"D'Artagnan! D'Artagnan!" she exclaimed. "Is it you?" This way!"

"Constance, Constance!" replied the young man. "Where are you? My God!"

At the same moment the door was burst in, rather than opened. Men rushed into the room. Madame Bonacieux had sunk into a chair without the power of moving. D'Artagnan cast away a still smoking pistol, and fell upon his knees before his mistress. Athos replaced his pistol in his belt; and Porthos and Aramis returned their drawn swords into their scabbards.

"Oh, d'Artagnan, my beloved d'Artagnan, you come at last! You did not deceive me, it is really you!"

"Yes, yes, Constance, we are at last united."

"Oh, how foolish *she* was to tell me that you would never come. I always secretly expected it. I did not want to flee. Oh, how wisely I have chosen! How happy I am!"

At this word, *she,* Athos, who had quietly sat down, suddenly arose.

"*She*? Who is *she*?" demanded d'Artagnan.

"My friend. Ah, I remember her name now; they mentioned it before me," said Madame Bonacieux. "Lady de Winter."

The four friends uttered one unanimous cry, but the voice of Athos overpowered all the others.

"Madame," said Athos, "whose empty glass is this?"

"Mine, sir," said the young woman in a dying voice. At the same moment she became livid; a deadly spasm assailed her; she sank panting into the arms of Porthos and Aramis.

D'Artagnan grasped the hand of Athos in indescribable anguish. "Ah," said he, "do you believe—" His voice was choked by sobs.

"I believe the worst," replied Athos.

"D'Artagnan' exclaimed Madame Bonacieux, "where are you? Do not leave me—you see that I am about to die!"

D'Artagnan let fall Athos's hands, which he had pressed convulsively, and ran to her. Her countenance, before so beautiful, was entirely distorted; her glassy eyes no longer saw, a convulsive shuddering agitated her whole frame; and icy drops streamed from her brow. "In the name of Heaven, run—. Aramis—Porthos—and call for help!"

"Useless!" said Athos. "All is useless! To the poison which she pours, there is no antidote."

"Yes, yes—help, help!" murmured Madame Bonacieux. Then collecting all her strength, she took the head of the young man between her two hands, looked him for an instant as though her whole soul was in that last look, and with a sobbing cry she pressed her lips upon his.

"Constance! Constance!" exclaimed d'Artagnan.

One sigh came from her lips breathing over those of d'Artagnan; and that sigh was the passage of her loving soul to eternity.

D'Artagnan held only a lifeless body in his arms. He uttered a cry and fell beside his mistress, as pale and motionless as herself.

Porthos wept, Aramis raised his hand to heaven, Athos made the sign of the cross.

At that moment a man appeared at the door, almost as pale as those who were in the room. He looked around him, and saw Madame Bonacieux dead, and d'Artagnan unconscious. He entered just at the moment of that stupor which succeeds great catastrophes.

"Gentlemen," said the newcomer, "you, like myself, are seeking a woman, who," added he, with a terrible smile, must have been present here for I see a corpse. Since you will not recognize a man whose life you have probably twice saved, I must name myself. I am Lord de Winter, that woman's brother-in-law."

The three friends uttered an exclamation of surprise. Athos arose and offered him his hand.

"Welcome, my lord," said he, "you are one of us."

"I left Portsmouth five hours after her," said Lord de Winter, "reached Boulogne three hours after her; I only missed her by twenty minutes at St. Omer; but at Lillers I lost trace of her. I wandered about on chance, inquiring of everybody, when I saw you pass at a gallop. I recognized M. d'Artagnan, and called out to you, but you did not answer me. I attempted to keep up with you but my horse was too tired to go at the same pace as yours did; and yet in spite of all your haste, it seems that you, too, arrived too late."

"The proof is before you," said Athos, pointing to Madame Bonacieux, lying dead, and to d'Artagnan, whom Porthos and Aramis were endeavouring to restore to consciousness.

"Are they both dead?" inquired Lord de Winter coldly.

"No, happily," replied Athos; "M. d'Artagnan has only fainted."

In fact, at that moment, d'Artagnan opened his eyes. He tore himself from the arms of Porthos and Aramis, and threw himself like a madman on the body of his mistress.

Athos arose, walked towards his friend with a slow and solemn step, embraced him tenderly, and then, whilst d'Artagnan broke out into sobs, said to him, in his noble and persuasive tones:

"My friend, be a man! Women weep for the dead—men avenge them!"

"Oh, yes, yes!" cried d'Artagnan. "If it be to avenge her, I am ready to follow you."

Athos took advantage of this momentary strength, which the hope of vengeance had given to his unfortunate friend, to make a sign to Porthos and Aramis to fetch the abbess.

The two friends met her in the corridor, in great agitation at such events. She called some of the sisters, who, contrary to their conventual habits, found themselves in the presence of five men.

"Madame," said Athos, putting his arm under that of d'Artagnan, "we leave to your pious care the body of this unfortunate woman. She was an angel upon earth before she became a saint in heaven. Treat her as if she had been one of your sisters: we will return some day to pray for her soul."

All five, followed by their servants leading their horses, then went towards the town of Béthune, whose suburbs were in sight; and they stopped at the first hotel they found.

"Now, gentlemen," said Athos, when he had ascertained that there were five unoccupied rooms in the hotel, "I take charge of everything; do not worry."

"It seems to me, however," said Lord de Winter, "that if any measures are to be taken against the countess, the concern is mine, seeing that she is my sister-in-law."

"Mine also," said Athos; "she is my wife."

D'Artagnan started, for he knew that Athos was sure of his revenge, to reveal such a secret. Porthos and Aramis looked at one another in consternation; and Lord de Winter thought that Athos had gone mad.

"Retire, then," said Athos, "and leave me to act. You see that in my capacity of husband, this affair belongs to me. Only, d'Artagnan, if you have not lost it, give me that paper which fell from the man's hat, and on which the name of a village is written."

"Ah!" cried d'Artagnan. "I understand: that name is written by her hand.—"

"You see," said Athos, "that there is still a God in heaven."

Athos's despair had given place to a concentrated grief which made the brilliant qualities of the man even keener. He requested the landlord to bring him a map of the province; and then he bent himself over it, and perceiving that four different roads led from Béthune to Armentières he ordered the valets to be called.

Planchet, Grimaud, Mousqueton and Bazin entered, and received Athos's clear, precise and serious directions. At break of day, the next morning, they were to set off and proceed to Armentières, each by a different road. Planchet, the most intelligent of the four, was to follow that which had been taken by the carriage at which the four friends had fired, and which was accompanied, as may be remembered, by Rochefort's lackey.

They were all four to meet at an appointed place the next day, at eleven o'clock. If they had discovered her ladyship's retreat, three of the four were to remain to watch her, and the fourth was to return to Béthune, to inform Athos and to guide the four friends.

Athos then girded on his sword, wrapped himself up in his cloak, and left the hotel. It was about ten o'clock; and at ten at night in the provinces, the streets are but little frequented. Nevertheless, he was visibly eager to find someone of whom he could ask a question

At length he met a belated passer-by, and went up and spoke to him. He and everyone else he asked started back in fear when they knew his destination, but a travelling beggar went with him for a piece of silver. He pointed out, at a distance, a small, isolated, melancholy-looking house, to which Athos proceeded; whilst the beggar, who had received his fee, hurried away as fast as he could.

Athos walked quite round this house before he could distinguish the door from the reddish colour in which the hut was painted. No light pierced through the chinks of the shutters; no sound gave reason to suppose it was inhabited; it was sad and silent as a tomb. Athos knocked three times before any answer was returned.

A man of tall stature and pale complexion, and with black beard and hair, appeared. Athos exchanged a few words with him in a whisper, and then the tall man made a sign to the musketeer that he might enter. Athos immediately availed himself of the permission, and the door closed behind him.

The man took him into a laboratory, where he was engaged in joining together with iron wires the clattering bones of a skeleton. All the body was already adjusted, and the head alone was lying on the table. All the furniture indicated that the owner of the room in which they were was engaged in natural science. But there was no family, no servant: the tall man lived alone in this house.

Athos explained the cause of his visit and the service he required; but scarcely had he stated his demand when the man started back in fright, and refused. Athos then took from his pocket a small paper, on which two lines and a signature were written, accompanied by a seal, and presented it to him who had shown these signs of repugnance so prematurely. The tall man had scarcely read the two lines, seen the signature, and recognized the seal, when he bowed as a token that he had no longer any objection to make, and that he was prepared to obey. Athos demanded nothing more: he arose, left the house, returned by the road he had come, and re-entering the hotel shut himself up in his own room.

At daybreak, d'Artagnan entered his room, and asked him what they were to do.

"Wait," replied Athos.

The four friends, with Lord de Winter, first attended the funeral of poor Constance Bonacieux. After the service, Athos searched the garden, and following her tracks and bloodstains on the road discovered where a carriage had waited for the poisoner, and what road she had taken to escape.

Satisfied with this discovery which confirmed all his conjectures, Athos returned to the hotel, where Planchet was patiently awaiting him. He had gone farther than Athos; so that in the village of Festubert, whilst drinking in a tavern, he had, without the trouble of inquiry, learned that at half-past eight the evening before, a wounded man, who attended a lady travelling in a post-carriage, had- been obliged to stop, from inability to proceed farther. The accident had been imputed to robbers, who had stopped the carriage in the wood. The man had remained in the village, but the woman had changed horses, and proceeded on her journey.

Planchet hunted out the postillion who had driven the carriage, and found him. He had taken the lady to Fromelles and from there she had gone on to Armentières. Planchet had taken a short cut, and at half-past seven in the morning he was at Armentières. There was only one hotel there and Planchet presented himself at it as a servant who was looking for a situation. He had not talked ten minutes with the servants at the inn, before he ascertained that a woman had arrived alone at eleven o'clock the night before, had hired a room, had sent for the landlord, and had told him that she wished to remain for some time in the neighbourhood. Planchet needed to know nothing more. He hastened to the place of appointment, found the three other valets at their posts, placed them as sentinels at all the exits from the hotel, and returned to Athos, who was just hearing the last of this information from Planchet when his friends returned.

All their faces were sombre and anxious even the gentle countenance of Aramis.

"What are we to do?" said d'Artagnan.

"Wait!" replied Athos.

Each returned to his own room.

At eight o'clock in the evening, Athos ordered the horses to be saddled, and sent word to Lord de Winter and his friends to prepare for the expedition. In an instant the five were ready. Each looked at his arms and put them in order. Athos came down last, and found d'Artagnan already mounted and impatient.

"Patience," said Athos, "there is still one of us missing."

The four horsemen looked around them in astonishment, for they wondered in vain who this could be.

At this moment Planchet led up Athos's horse. The musketeer leapt lightly into the saddle.

"Wait for me," he said, "I shall be back directly." And he went off at a gallop.

A quarter of an hour afterwards he returned, accompanied by a man who wore a mask, and was wrapped in a red cloak. Lord de Winter and the three musketeers questioned each other with glances, but none of them could give any information to the others, for all were ignorant who this man was. And yet they concluded that this was as it ought to be, since it was Athos who had so arranged it.

At nine o'clock, guided by Planchet, the little cavalcade began its march, taking the same road that the carriage had followed.

They passed in silence through the village of Festubert, where the wounded servant had been left. Having reached Herlies, Planchet, who guided the party, turned to the left.

On several occasions either Lord de Winter, or Porthos, or Aramis had tried to address some remark to the man in the red cloak; but at each interrogation he had bowed his head without reply. The travellers had thus understood that there must be some reason for the stranger's silence, and they had ceased to address him.

A little way beyond Fromelles a storm broke upon them. There were still three leagues to travel and they rode amid torrents of rain. At the moment that the little troop had passed beyond Goskal, and was just arriving at the posting house, a man, who in the darkness had been confounded with the trunk of a tree under which he was sheltering, advanced into the middle of the road, placing his finger on his lips.

Athos recognized Grimaud.

"What is the matter now?" exclaimed d'Artagnan. "Can she have left Armentières?"

Grimaud nodded.

"Where is she?" demanded Athos.

Grimaud pointed in the direction of the River Lys.

"Far from here?"

Grimaud presented his forefinger bent.

"Alone?" demanded Athos.

Grimaud made a sign that she was.

"Gentlemen?" said Athos, "she is alone, half a league from here, in the direction of the river."

"Good," said d'Artagnan, "lead us on, Grimaud."

Grimaud set off across country, and guided the cavalcade. At the end of about five hundred yards they came to a stream, which they forded. By the light of a flash, they perceived the village of Erquinghem.

"Is it there?" demanded d'Artagnan.

Grimaud shook his head.

The troop proceeded on its way. Another flash blazed forth; and by its bluish glare a small solitary house was perceptible on the bank of the river not far from the ferry. There was a light at one window.

"We are there," said Athos.

At that moment a man who was lying down in a ditch, jumped up. It was Mousqueton. He pointed with his finger to the window with the light. "She is there," said he.

"And Bazin?" demanded Athos.

"While I watched the window, he watched the door."

"Good," said Athos; "you are all faithful servants."

Athos leapt from his horse, gave the bridle to Grimaud, and advanced towards the window, after having made a sign to the rest of the troop to go towards the door. The little house was surrounded by a quickset hedge two or three feet high. Athos sprang over the hedge and went up to the window, which had no shutters on the outside, but whose short curtains were closely drawn. By the light of a lamp he could perceive a woman, wrapped in a dark-coloured cloak seated on a stool before an expiring fire. Her elbows were resting upon a mean table, and she leant her head on her hands which were white as ivory. Her face was not visible, but an ominous smile arose upon Athos's lips. He was not mistaken. He had in truth found the woman that he sought.

At this moment a horse neighed. Her ladyship raised her head, saw the pale face of Athos staring through the window, and screamed aloud.

Perceiving that he had been seen, Athos pushed the window with his hand and knee. It gave way, the panes were broken, and Athos, like a spectre of vengeance, leapt into the room. Her ladyship ran to the door and opened it. Paler, and even more threatening than Athos himself d'Artagnan was standing on the sill. My lady started back and screamed. D'Artagnan, imagining that she had some means of flight, and fearing that she might escape them, drew a pistol from his belt. But Athos raised his hand.

"Replace your weapon, d'Artagnan," said he; "it is imperative that this woman should be judged, and not assassinated. Wait awhile, d'Artagnan, and you shall be satisfied. Come in, gentlemen."

D'Artagnan obeyed; for Athos had the solemn voice and the authoritative air of a judge commissioned by the Deity Himself. Behind d'Artagnan, there came Porthos, Aramis, Lord de Winter, and the man in the red cloak. The four valets watched at the door and window. Her ladyship had sunk upon her seat, with her hands stretched out, as if to exorcise this terrible apparition. On seeing her brother-in-law she uttered a fearful scream.

"What do you want?" she cried.

"We want," said Athos, "Anne de Breuil, Charlotte Backson, who was called first the Countess de la Fère, then Lady de Winter, Baroness of Sheffield."

"I am that person," murmured she, overwhelmed with terror. "What do you want with me?"

"We want to judge you according to your crimes," said Athos. "You will be free to defend yourself; and to justify your conduct if you can. M. d'Artagnan, you must be the first accuser."

D'Artagnan came forward. "Before God and men," said he, "I accuse this woman of having poisoned Constance Bonacieux, who died last night." He turned towards Aramis and Porthos.

"We can bear witness to it," said the two musketeers together.

D'Artagnan continued:

"Before God and before men, I accuse this woman of having sought to poison me with wine, which she sent me from Villeroi, with a forged letter as if the wine had come from my friends. God preserved me, but a man named Brisemont died instead of me."

"We bear witness to this," said Porthos and Aramis as with one voice.

"Before God and men," continued d'Artagnan, "I accuse this woman of having urged me to murder the Baron de Wardes; and as no one is present to bear witness to it, I myself will attest it. I have done."

And d'Artagnan crossed over the other side of the room with Porthos and Aramis.

"It is now for you to speak, my lord," said Athos.

The baron came forward in his turn. "Before God and before men," said he, "I accuse this woman of having caused the Duke of Buckingham to be assassinated."

"The Duke of Buckingham assassinated!" cried all, with one accord.

"Yes," said the baron, "assassinated! From the warning letter which you sent me, I caused this woman to be arrested, and put her under the custody of a faithful dependant. She corrupted that man, she placed the dagger in his hand; she made him kill the duke; and at this moment, perhaps Felton has paid with his head for the crimes of his fury."

A shudder ran through the company at the revelation of these hitherto unsuspected crimes.

"This is not all," resumed Lord de Winter. "My brother, who had made you his heiress, died in three hours of a strange malady, which left livid spots on his body. Sister, how did your husband die?"

"Oh, horror!" exclaimed Porthos and Aramis.

"Assassin of Buckingham, assassin of Felton, assassin of my

brother—I demand justice of you; and declare that if it be not accorded to me, I will execute it myself!"

Lord de Winter ranged himself by the side of d'Artagnan, leaving his place open to another accuser.

Her ladyship's head sank upon her hands, and she endeavoured to recall her thoughts, which were confounded by a deadly vertigo.

"It is now my turn," said Athos, trembling as the lion trembles at the aspect of a serpent. "It is my turn. I married this woman when she was a young girl. I married her against the wishes of all my family. I gave her my property; I gave her my name; and one day I discovered that this woman was branded—this woman bore the mark of a fleur-de-lis upon her left shoulder."

"Oh!" said her ladyship, rising "I defy you to find the tribunal which pronounced on me that infamous sentence—I defy you to find the man who executed it!"

"Silence!" exclaimed a voice. "It is for me to answer that!" And the man in the red cloak came forward, and took off his mask.

Every eye was turned towards him, for he was unknown to all except Athos.

Her ladyship looked for some time with increasing terror on that pale countenance, fringed with black hair, of which the only expression was that of a frozen sternness.

"But who are you?" exclaimed all the witnesses of this scene.

"Ask this woman," said the man in the red cloak, "for you see well that she has recognized me."

"The executioner of Lille! The executioner of Lille!" cried her ladyship, overcome by wild affright, and clinging to the wall with her hands for support.

The stranger paused for silence. "I told you truly that she recognized me," said he. "Yes, I am the executioner of Lille, and here is my history."

All eyes were fixed upon the man, whose words were listened to with the most anxious avidity.

"This woman was formerly a young girl, as beautiful as she is at present. She was a nun, in a Benedictine convent at Templemar. A young priest, simple and ingenuous in his nature, performed service in the church of the convent: she attempted to seduce him, and succeeded. She would have seduced a saint. The vows which they had both taken were sacred and irrevocable. She persuaded him to quit the country. But they required money. The priest stole the sacred vessels and sold them; but just as they were making ready to escape, they were both arrested. In eight days more she had corrupted the gaoler's son, and saved herself. The young priest was condemned to be branded, and to ten years in chains. I was the executioner of Lille, as this woman says. I was obliged to brand the criminal, and that criminal was my own brother! I then swore that this woman, who had ruined him— who was more than his accomplice since she had urged him to the crime—should at least share his punishment. I suspected where she was concealed. I followed and discovered her, I bound her and imprinted the same brand on her that I had stamped upon my own brother. The next day, on my return to Lille, my brother also managed to escape. I was accused as his accomplice, and was condemned to remain in prison in his place so long as he should continue at large. My poor brother was not aware of this sentence; he had rejoined this woman, and they fled together into Berry, where he obtained a small curacy. This woman passed for his sister. The owner of the estate to which the curacy belonged saw this pretended sister, and fell in love with her so deeply that he proposed to marry her. She left the man whom she had destroyed, and became the Countess de la Fère."

All eyes were turned upon Athos, whose true name this was, and he made a sign that the executioner's tale was true.

"Then," continued the latter, "my poor brother returned to Lille; and hearing the sentence which had condemned me in his place, he delivered himself up to justice, and hanged himself the same night to the grating of his dungeon. They who had condemned me kept their word. Scarcely was the identity of the dead body proved, before my liberty was restored. These are the crimes of which I accuse her—these are the reasons why I branded her!"

"M. d'Artagnan," said Athos, "what is the punishment that you demand for this woman?"

"The punishment of death!" replied d'Artagnan.

"My Lord de Winter," continued Athos, "what punishment do you demand for this woman?"

"Death!" replied his lordship

"Messieurs Porthos and Aramis," said Athos, "you who are her judges—what punishment do you pronounce against this woman?"

"The punishment of death!" replied the two musketeers, in a hollow voice.

Her ladyship uttered a fearful shriek, and dragged herself a few paces on her knees towards her judges.

Athos stretched out his hand towards her. "Charlotte Backson, Anne de Breuil," he said, "Countess de la Fère, Lady de Winter, your crimes have wearied men on earth and God in heaven. If you know any prayer, repeat it; for you are condemned and are about to die."

At these words, which left no hope, her ladyship raised herself to her full height, and attempted to speak. But her voice failed her. She felt a strong and pitiless hand seize her by the hair, and drag her on, as irresistibly as Fate drags on mankind. She did not, therefore, even attempt to make any resistance, but went out of the cottage.

Lord de Winter and the four friends went out after her. The valets followed their masters, and the chamber was left empty, with its broken window, its open door, and the smoking lamp burning sadly on the table.

It was almost midnight. The waning moon, as red as blood from the lingering traces of the storm, was rising behind the little village of Armentières. In front the Lys rolled along its waters like a river of molten fire.

Two of the servants, each holding an arm, led her ladyship along. The executioner walked behind. The four musketeers and Lord de Winter followed him in turn. Planchet and Bazin brought up the rear.

The two valets led her ladyship towards the bank of the river. Her mouth was mute, but her eyes were inexpressibly eloquent, supplicating by turns each of those on whom she looked. Finding herself a few paces in advance, she whispered to the valets:

"A thousand pistoles for each of you, if you will assist me to escape; but if you give me up to your masters, I have some avengers near, who will make you pay dearly for my death."

Grimaud hesitated and Mousqueton trembled in every limb.

Athos, who had heard her ladyship's voice, came up immediately, as did also Lord de Winter.

"Send away those valets," said he; "she has spoken to them and they are no longer to be trusted."

They called Planchet and Bazin, who took the places of Grimaud and Mousqueton.

Having reached the brink of the stream, the executioner came up, and bound her ladyship's hands and feet.

Then she broke her silence to exclaim—"You are cowards, you are miserable assassins! You come, ten of you, to murder one poor woman! But beware, though I am not assisted, I shall be avenged!"

"You are not a woman," replied Athos coldly; "you do not belong to the human race; you are a demon escaped from hell, and to hell we shall send you back."

"Oh, you stainless gentleman," said her ladyship, "remember that he amongst you who touches a hair of my head is himself a murderer!"

"The executioner can kill, without being on that account a murderer, madame," said the man in the cloak. "He is the last judge on earth—that is all."

Her ladyship uttered a scream of terror and fell upon her knees. The executioner lifted her in his arms, and prepared to carry her to the boat.

D'Artagnan's heart failed him. "I cannot consent that this woman should die thus!"

But Athos drew his sword. "If you take one step farther, d'Artagnan," he said, "we cross swords. Come, executioner, do your duty!"

"Willingly, my lord," replied the executioner, "for as truly as I am a good Catholic, I firmly believe that I act justly in exercising my office on this woman."

"That is right." Athos took one step towards her ladyship. "I pardon you," said he, "the evil you have done me. I forgive you for my future crushed, my honour lost, my love tainted, and my salvation for ever imperiled, by the despair into which you have thrown me. Die in peace!"

Lord de Winter next came forward. "I pardon you," said he, "the poisoning of my brother, the assassination of the Duke of Buckingham, and the death of poor Felton. I forgive you your attempts on my own person. Die in peace!"

"As for me," said d'Artagnan, "pardon me, madame, for having by a deceit unworthy of a gentleman provoked your rage; and in exchange I pardon you for the murder of my poor friend, and your cruel vengeance on myself. I pardon and I weep for you. Die in peace!"

"I am lost," murmured her ladyship in English; "I must die!" She threw around her one of those clear glances, which seemed to emanate from an eye of fire. But she saw nothing. She listened; but she heard nothing. There were none around but her enemies. "Where am I to die?" she demanded.

"On the other bank," replied the executioner. He then placed her in the boat.

"Mark," said Athos, "this woman has a child, and yet she has not said one word about him."

The boat proceeded towards the left bank of the Lys, carrying away the criminal and the executioner. All the others remained on the right bank, where they had sunk upon their knees. The boat glided slowly along the ferryrope, under the reflection of a pale mist, which hung over the water at that moment. It arrived at the other bank, and the two figures stood out in blackness on the red horizon.

Then from the other shore, they could see the executioner slowly raise his two arms, a ray of the moon was reflected on the blade of his sword, the two arms descended, they heard the whistling of the scimitar and the victim's cry; and then a truncated mass sank down beneath the blow. The executioner took off his red cloak, stretched it out on the ground, laid the body on it and threw in the head, tied it by the four corners, swung it upon his shoulders, and again entered the boat. Having reached the middle of the Lys, he stopped the boat, and holding his burden over the river—

"Let the justice of God have its course!" he exclaimed in a loud voice. And so saying, he dropped the dead body into the deepest part of the waters, which closed above it.

13

Even the Cardinal is Moved

Three days afterwards, the four musketeers returned to Paris. They were within the limit of their leave of absence, and, the same evening, they went to pay the usual visit to M. de Tréville.

"Well, gentlemen," inquired the brave captain, "have you enjoyed your excursion?"

"Prodigiously," replied Athos, in his own name and that of his companions.

On the sixth of the following month, the king, according to his promise to the cardinal to return to La Rochelle, quitted Paris, still quite stunned by the news which was beginning to circulate in the city, that Buckingham had been assassinated.

The queen refused to give credence to the fatal news until La Poste arrived from England, bringing with him the last dying gift which Buckingham sent to her. The king's joy was extreme. He did not take the slightest pains to disguise it, but displayed it affectedly before the queen. Louis XIII, like all men of weak mind, was wanting in generosity. But he soon became melancholy and ill again. His brow was not one of those that can continue long unruffled; he felt that in returning to the camp, he returned to slavery.

The return to La Rochelle, was therefore, profoundly melancholy. Our four friends, especially, excited the astonishment of their companions: they travelled side by side, with heavy eyes and hanging heads.

One day, when the king had halted to hunt the magpie, and the four friends, instead of joining in the sport, had stopped at a tavern by the roadside, a man, who was coming post-haste from La Rochelle, stopped at the door to drink a glass of wine and looked into the room where the four musketeers were sitting at a table.

"M. d'Artagnan," said he, "is it you that I see there?"

D'Artagnan raised his head, and uttered a cry of joy. It was his phantom: the stranger of Meung, of the Rue des Fossoyeurs, and of Arras. D'Artagnan drew his sword and rushed towards the door. But on this occasion, the stranger, instead of hastening away, jumped off his horse and advanced to meet him.

"Ah, sir," said the young man, "I meet you at last. This time you shall not escape me."

"It is not my intention either, sir; for I am looking for you this time. In the king's name, I arrest you!"

"What do you mean?" exclaimed d'Artagnan.

"I say you must give up your sword to me, sir, and without resistance. Your life depends upon it. I warn you."

"But who are you?" demanded d'Artagnan, lowering his sword, but not yet giving it up.

"I am the Chevalier de Rochefort," said the stranger, "Cardinal Richelieu's master of the horse, and I am commanded to conduct you before his Eminence."

"We are now returning to his Eminence, sir," said Athos, coming forward, "and you must take M. d'Artagnan's word that he will go direct to La Rochelle."

"I must place him in the hands of the guards, who will conduct him back to the camp."

"We will serve as his guards, sir, on our words as gentlemen! But on our words as gentlemen, also," continued Athos, frowning, "M. d'Artagnan shall not be taken from us."

De Rochefort threw a glance behind him, and saw that Porthos and Aramis had placed themselves between him and the door; and he understood that he was entirely at the mercy of these four men.

"Gentlemen," said he, "if M. d'Artagnan will deliver up his sword, and add his word to yours, I will be contented with your promise of conducting him to his Eminence's quarters."

"You have my word, sir, and here is my sword," said d'Artagnan.

"That suits me all the better," said Rochefort, "as I must continue my journey."

"If it is to rejoin her ladyship," said Athos coolly, "it is useless; you will not find her."

"And what has become of her?" asked Rochefort anxiously.

"Return to the camp, and you will learn!"

Rochefort remained in thought for an instant; and then, as they were only one day's journey from Surgères, where the cardinal was to meet the king, he resolved to follow Athos's advice, and to return with them.

The next day, at three in the afternoon, they reached Surgères. The cardinal was waiting there for Louis XIII. The minister and the king congratulated each other on the happy chance which had freed France from the inveterate enemy who was arming Europe against her.

On returning in the evening to his quarters, the cardinal found the three musketeers all armed, and d'Artagnan, without his sword, standing in front of the house which he occupied. On this occasion, as he had all his retinue with him, he looked sternly at them, and made a sign with his eye and hand for d'Artagnan to follow him. D'Artagnan obeyed.

"We will wait for you, d'Artagnan," said Athos, loud enough for the cardinal to hear.

D'Artagnan entered behind the cardinal, and Rochefort followed d'Artagnan: the door was guarded. His Eminence entered a room, and signed to Rochefort to bring in the young musketeer. Rochefort obeyed, and retired.

D'Artagnan stood alone before the cardinal. It was his second interview with Richelieu; and he afterwards confessed that he felt quite convinced that it was to be his last. Richelieu remained leaning against the chimney-piece. A table stood between him and d'Artagnan.

"Sir," said the cardinal, "you have been arrested by my orders."

"So I have been informed, my lord."

"Do you know why?"

"No, my lord; for the only thing for which I ought to be arrested is yet unknown to your Eminence."

Richelieu looked earnestly at the young man "What does this mean?" he said.

"If your Eminence will first tell me the charges against me I will then tell you what I have done."

"You are accused of corresponding with the enemies of the realm; of having pried into the secrets of the state; and of having attempted to make your general's plans miscarry."

"And who is my accuser, my lord?" inquired d'Artagnan who had no doubt that it was her ladyship. "A woman branded by the law of her country—a woman who was married to one man in France, and to another in England—a woman who poisoned her second husband, and attempted to poison me!"

"What are you saying, sir," exclaimed the astonished cardinal, "and of what woman are you speaking?"

"Of Lady de Winter," replied d'Artagnan; "yes, of Lady de Winter—of whose crimes your Eminence was undoubtedly ignorant, when you honoured her with your confidence."

"Sir," said the cardinal, "if Lady de Winter has been guilty of the crimes you have mentioned, she shall be punished."

"She has been punished, my lord!"

"And who has punished her?"

"We have."

"She is in prison, then?"

"She is dead."

"Dead!" repeated the cardinal, who could not credit what he heard. "Dead! Did you say that she was dead?"

Three times she tried to kill me, and three times I forgave her;

but she murdered the woman I loved; and then my friends and I seized her, tried her and condemned her." D'Artagnan then related the poisoning of Madame Bonacieux in the Carmelite convent at Béthune, the trial in the solitary house, and the execution on the banks of the Lys.

A shudder ran through the frame of the cardinal, who was not made to shudder easily. "So," said he, in a voice, the gentleness of which contrasted strangely with the severity of his words, "you constituted yourselves the judges, forgetting that those who are not legally appointed and punish without authority, are assassins. You are a man of courage, sir, but I tell you now that you will be tried and even condemned."

"Another might reply to your Eminence that he had his pardon in his pocket. I content myself with saying—command, my lord, and I am ready."

"Your pardon!" said Richelieu, in surprise.

"Yes, my lord," replied d'Artagnan.

"And signed by whom? By the king?" The cardinal pronounced these words with a singular intonation of contempt.

"No; by your Eminence."

"By me? You are mad, sir!"

"Your Eminence will undoubtedly recognize your own writing." And d'Artagnan presented to the cardinal the precious paper which Athos had extorted from her ladyship, and which he had given to d'Artagnan as a safeguard.

The cardinal took the paper, and read in a very slow voice, and lingering over each syllable:

> It is by my order, and for the good of the state, that the bearer
> of this has done what he has done.
> Richelieu.

The cardinal, after having read these two lines fell into a profound reverie, but did not return the paper to d'Artagnan.

"He is deciding by what kind of punishment I am to die," said the Gascon to himself "Well, faith! He shall see how a gentleman can die." The young musketeer was in an excellent frame of mind for ending his career heroically.

Richelieu continued to meditate, rolling and unrolling the paper in his hand. At last he raised his head, and fixed his eagle eye upon that open, loyal and intelligent countenance, and read upon that face, all furrowed with tears, the sufferings that d'Artagnan had endured for a month; and he then thought for the third or fourth time what the future might have in store for such a youth, of barely twenty years of age, and what resources his activity, courage and intelligence might offer to a good master. On the other side, her ladyship's crimes, her power of mind, her almost infernal genius had more than once alarmed him; and he felt a secret joy at being for ever freed from such a dangerous accomplice. He slowly tore up the paper which d'Artagnan had so generously presented him.

"I am lost," said d'Artagnan, in his own heart.

The cardinal approached the table, and without sitting down, wrote some words on a parchment, of which two thirds were already filled up, and then affixed his seal.

"That is my condemnation," thought d'Artagnan; "he spares me the misery of the Bastille and the delays of a trial. That is really kind of him."

"Here, sir," said the cardinal to the young man; "I took one *carte blanche* from you, and I give you another. The name is not inserted in the commission; you will add it yourself."

It was the commission of a lieutenant in the musketeers

D'Artagnan fell at the cardinal's feet. "My lord," said he; my life is yours—make use of it henceforth; but this favour which you bestow upon me is beyond my merits. I have three friends who are more worthy of it."

"You are a brave youth, d'Artagnan," said the cardinal, tapping him familiarly on the shoulder, in his delight in having conquered that rebellious nature. "Do what you like with this commission as it is blank; only remember that it is to you I give it."

"Your Eminence may rest assured," said d'Artagnan, "th will never forget it."

The cardinal turned, and said aloud: "Rochefort!"

The chevalier, who had undoubtedly been behind the door, immediately entered.

"Rochefort," said the cardinal, "you see M. d'Artagnan: I receive him into the number of my friends. Embrace one another, and be prudent if you wish to retain your heads."

D'Artagnan and Rochefort embraced coldly, but the cardinal was watching them with his vigilant eye. They left the room at the same moment.

"We shall meet again," they both said, "shall we not?"

"Whenever you please," said d'Artagnan.

"The time will come," said Rochefort.

"Hum!" said Richelieu, opening the door.

The two men bowed to his Eminence, smiled, and pressed each other's hands.

"We began to be impatient," said Athos.

"Here I am, my friends," replied d'Artagnan. "Not only free, but in favour."

"You must tell us all about it."

"Yes, this evening. But, for the present, let us separate."

In fact, in the evening, d'Artagnan went to Athos's lodgings, and found him emptying a bottle of Spanish wine, an occupation which he pursued religiously every night. He told him all that had taken place between the cardinal and himself, and drew the commission from his pocket.

"Here, dear Athos," said he, "here is something which naturally belongs to you."

Athos smiled his soft and gentle smile. "Friend," said he, "for Athos it is too much—for the Count de la Fère it is too little. Keep this commission, it belongs to you. Alas! You have bought it dearly enough!"

D'Artagnan left Athos's room and went to Porthos's.

He found him clothed in a most magnificent coat covered in splendid embroidery, and admiring himself in a mirror.

"Ah! It is you, my friend," said Porthos; "how do you think this outfit suits me?"

"Beautifully," replied d'Artagnan; "but I am going to offer you one which will suit you still more."

"What is it?" demanded Porthos.

"That of a lieutenant of the musketeers," and d'Artagnan, having related to Porthos his interview with the cardinal, drew the commission from his pocket. "Here," said he, "fill in your name and be a kind officer to me."

Porthos glanced over the commission and returned it, to the great astonishment of the young man.

"Yes," said Porthos, "that would flatter me very much, but I could not long enjoy the favour. During our expedition to Béthune, the husband of my duchess died; so that, my dear boy, the strong-box of the defunct is holding out its arms to me; I am going to marry the widow. You see I am fitting on my wedding garments. So keep the lieutenancy, my dear fellow, keep it," and he returned it to d'Artagnan.

The young man then repaired to Aramis. He found him kneeling before an oratory, with his forehead leaning on an open book of prayers. He told him, also, of his interview with the cardinal, and taking his commission from his pocket for the third time, said:

"You, our friend, our light, our invisible protector, accept this commission: you have merited it more than anybody by your wisdom and your counsels, always followed by such fortunate results."

"Alas, dear friend," said Aramis, "our last adventures have entirely disgusted me with the military life! My decision is, this time, irrevocable. After the siege, I shall enter the Lazarists. Keep the commission d'Artagnan. The profession of arms suits you: you will be a brave and adventurous captain."

D'Artagnan, with an eye moist with gratitude, and brilliant with joy, returned to Athos, whom he found still seated at the table, admiring his last glass of Malaga by the light of his lamp.

"Well," said he, "they have both refused it."

"It is, dear friend, because no one is more worthy of it than yourself." Athos took a pen, wrote the name of d'Artagnan upon the paper and gave it back to him.

"I shall no longer have my friends, then," said the young man. "Alas! Nothing, henceforth, but bitter recollections." And he let his head fall between his hands, whilst two tears rolled along his cheeks.

"You are young," said Athos, "and your bitter recollections have time to change themselves to tender remembrances."

Epilogue

La Rochelle, deprived of the assistance of the English fleet and of the succour that had been promised by Buckingham, surrendered after a year's siege. On the 28th October, 1628, the capitulation was signed.

The king entered Paris on the 23rd December of the same year. He was received in triumph as though he had conquered an enemy instead of Frenchmen.

D'Artagnan took his promotion. Porthos quitted the service and married Madame Coquenard during the following year. The strong-box, so much coveted, contained eight hundred thousand livres. Mousqueton had a superb livery, and enjoyed his lifelong dream of riding behind a gilded carriage

Aramis, after a journey to Lorraine, suddenly disappeared and ceased to write to his friends. They learned afterwards through Madame de Chevreuse, that he had assumed the cowl in a monastery at Nancy. Bazin became a lay-brother.

Athos remained a musketeer, under d'Artagnan's command, until 1633; at which time, after a journey to Touraine, he also left the service, under the pretext of having succeeded to a small family property in Roussillon. Grimaud followed Athos.

D'Artagnan fought three times with Rochefort; and wounded him three times.

"I shall probably kill you the fourth time," said he to Rochefort, as he stretched forth a hand to help him to rise.

"It would be better for us both to stop here," replied the

wounded man. "Vive Dieu! I have been more your friend than you think; for after our first meeting I could have got your head cut off by one word to the cardinal."

They embraced, but this time it was in sincerity, and without malice.

Planchet obtained, through Rochefort, the rank of sergeant in the regiment of Piedmont.

M. Bonacieux lived on very quietly, entirely ignorant of what had become of his wife, and caring little about it. One day he had the imprudence to recall himself to the cardinal's memory. The cardinal told him that he would so provide for him that he would never want for anything in the future. In fact, the next day, M. Bonacieux left his home at seven o'clock in the evening to go to the Louvre, and was never seen again in the Rue des Fossoyeurs. The opinion of those who thought themselves the best informed was that he was fed and lodged in some royal castle, at the expense of his generous Eminence.

Also available in

Treasure Island

R.L. Stevenson

Robert Louis Stevenson (1850-94) was born in
Scotland and journeyed widely, from Spain to
the California gold-fields, finally settling in
Samoa, where he died. By then he was
recognized as one of the greatest story tellers
ever, and *Treasure Island* has become one of the
world's best-loved adventure stories.

The story begins with a mysterious treasure
map and an old buccaneer in an English country
inn: soon we are on the high seas in a dangerous
Caribbean quest that becomes a desperate battle
of wits between young Jim Hawkins and the
unforgettable wily old pirate Long John Silver.

As the tension mounts, who will be first to
find the dead man's chest and its fabulous
treasure?

Also available in

The Call of the Wild

Jack London

Jack London (1876-1916) was born in San Francisco and grew up on the waterfront of Oakland. Much of his youth was spent on the wrong side of the law.

He joined the Klondike gold rush in 1897, returning to Oakland to write about his experiences there.

The Call of The Wild is the story of Buck, half St Bernard, half sheepdog, stolen from his comfortable Californian home and taken to the Klondike as a sled dog.

How Buck learns to endure and to be free is inspiringly told in Jack London's classic story of survival.

Also available in

Uncle Tom's Cabin

Harriet Beecher Stowe

Harriet Elizabeth Beecher Stowe, authoress of *Uncle Tom's Cabin*, was born at Lichfield, Connecticut, USA, in 1812.

Uncle Tom's Cabin, which is a direct attack upon the system of slavery that then existed in the Southern States, was first published in serial form in 1851–52. It became immediately famous, was translated into many foreign languages, and has since been published in innumerable editions. It did much to form public opinion in the United States against slavery, which was ultimately abolished as a result of the war between the Northern and Southern States in 1861–65.

Also available in

A Christmas Carol & Cricket on the Hearth

Charles Dickens

Charles Dickens, probably the best known and most popular English novelist, was born at Portsmouth in 1812. He suffered many hardships as a child and this probably resulted in him becoming an extremely hard worker for all his life. He published many novels dealing with the wrongs inflicted on children by adults in the 19th century.

A Christmas Carol was a sensational success when it was first published and he followed it in consecutive years with other Christmas books including *Cricket on the Hearth*, also contained in the same volume.

Also available in

Don Quixote

Miguel de Cervantes

For over three centuries, readers all over the world have been delighted by the adventures of Don Quixote and his squire Sancho Panza.

Children too should be introduced to the Quixotic idea and to the lasting charm, pathos and humour of Cervantes, contained in a new paperback volume.

Also available in

CHILDREN'S
CLASSICS

20,000 Leagues Under The Sea

Jules Verne

Jules Verne (1828–1905) was born in France and became the world's first great science fiction writer.

In his *20,000 Leagues Under the Sea*, an expedition led by Professor Aaronax tries to track down a sea monster that has been sinking ships all over the world. Their ship explodes and suddenly they are on board the 'sea monster', which turns out to be a submarine called *The Nautilus*, skippered by the mysterious Captain Nemo—an Indian Prince who has become the Robin Hood of the open seas, stealing gold to help the poor.

Verne's prophetic masterpiece of maritime adventures has fascinated every generation of readers since its publication in 1870.